Heartland

One Day You'll Know

"Walk on," Amy encouraged, putting her right hand around the filly's quarters and pressing lightly. Whenever she had seen her mom apply the same method, the foal had always walked forward. Not Daybreak: throwing her head high, she dug her heels in. Amy increased the pressure. "Walk on," she said more firmly.

With a speed that took Amy completely by surprise, Daybreak shot backwards. She reached the end of the lead-rope before Amy could release it from her hand. As the rope tightened and stopped her with a jerk, Daybreak gave an enraged squeal and rose on her back legs, her head fighting against the restraint, her front legs striking the air.

"Let go of the rope!" Ty shouted, looking round and seeing what was going on. "She'll go over, Amy!"

Heartland™

One Day You'll Know

Lauren Brooke

SCHOLASTIC

03174753

Scholastic Children's Books,
Commonwealth House, 1-19 New Oxford Street,
London WC1A 1NU, UK
a division of Scholastic Ltd
London ~ New York ~ Toronto ~ Sydney ~ Auckland
Mexico City ~ New Delhi ~ Hong Kong

Published in the UK by Scholastic Ltd, 2001
Series created by Working Partners Ltd

Heartland is a trademark of Working Partners Ltd

ISBN 0 439 99239 7

Typeset by TW Typesetting, Midsomer Norton, Somerset
Printed and bound by Nørhaven Paperback A/S, Denmark

8 10 9

With special thanks to Linda Chapman

To Mary Ritchie — a wonderful friend; who listens with her heart, not just her ears — just like Amy.

Chapter One

"Easy now," Amy Fleming murmured to Melody as the mare pulled against the long-line and whickered restlessly to her foal. Daybreak, the four-day-old filly, trotted inquisitively around the field, heedless of Melody's concern, her arched neck and intelligent head held high, her tiny hooves flicking lightly over the snow-covered grass. The pale November sun shone down on her bright chestnut coat. *The perfect Thanksgiving day…*

Amy held back her thoughts. No, she didn't want to think about it being Thanksgiving. That's why she was out here with Melody and Daybreak instead of being in the farmhouse with Grandpa and her older sister, Lou. That's why she'd been working non-stop on the yard all day. She didn't want to think about it being her first Thanksgiving without Mom.

Melody whinnied again.

"It's OK, girl," Amy said, her fingers moving in light circles on Melody's neck. "Your baby's safe. She's just taking a look around."

Registering the familiar, comforting touch of Amy's hands, Melody turned her head. Amy rubbed the mare's forehead and felt her relax slightly. *If you're here*, Melody seemed to be saying, *then everything must be OK*.

A warm glow spread through Amy as she saw the trust in the mare's eyes. Only a month ago, it had all been so different. When Melody had first arrived at Heartland, the horse sanctuary founded by Amy's late mother, she had been exceptionally wary. But gradually she came to trust Amy and, after Amy had assisted at Daybreak's birth, the bond between them seemed to deepen further.

An icy breeze blew Amy's long light-brown hair across her face. She pushed it back, her grey eyes moving towards the little foal. Every step the filly took looked so full of energy; it was hard to believe that just a few days ago they had feared for her life. Her birth had been difficult and for a while it had looked as though both mother and foal might die. However, Amy, Lou and Jack, their grandpa, had refused to give up – and, at long last, Daybreak had been born.

The filly stopped, her nostrils quivering, her beautiful proud head held high. As the rays of sun caught her coat, each chestnut hair seemed to flame brightly. Then the moment broke. With a toss of her head, Daybreak swung round. She cantered across the grass, butted her head hungrily underneath her mother's belly and began to drink.

Amy watched her short fluffy tail flicking from side to side and smiled. Ever since Daybreak's birth, she had felt an intense bond with the little foal. She wondered if it was just because she had been there at the filly's birth or whether it was something more than that. Her mom's voice came back to her: *Every so often, a special horse will come along — a horse that will touch your life for ever.* Looking at Daybreak, Amy was sure she knew what her mom had meant.

"Here, Daybreak," Amy murmured as the foal finished feeding. Daybreak took a step forward and sniffed Amy's outstretched hand, her intelligent eyes bright. "Good girl," Amy said softly, reaching to pat her neck.

With a squeal, Daybreak wheeled round. Amy jumped back just in time, gasping as the spirited filly kicked her back hooves cheekily into the air and cantered off.

A voice hailed Amy. "Looks like she's going to be a handful."

Amy swung round. Scott Trewin, the local equine vet, was standing at the gate with her sister, Lou.

"Scott!" she exclaimed. "What are you doing here?"

"Oh great," Scott teased. "I'm pleased to see you too, Amy."

"I didn't mean it like that," Amy grinned, going over. "I just thought you'd be at home with it being…" she struggled with the word "…Thanksgiving and all."

"He came to wish us a happy holiday, didn't you?" Lou said, turning to smile at Scott.

He took her hand and smiled back down at her. "Well, I couldn't *not* see you, could I?"

For a moment, Amy thought they were going to kiss. "OK – enough," she said hurriedly. Scott and Lou had recently started dating and, although she was delighted about it, there were limits to what she could stand!

Scott and Lou pulled apart – Scott grinning, Lou inspecting the tassels on her scarf. "So ... um, how's Daybreak today?" Lou asked Amy, her embarrassment emphasizing her English accent.

"Crazy," Amy replied, thinking, not for the first time, about how different she and her sister sounded. Whereas Lou had lived nearly all her life in England, Amy had moved to Virginia when she was three. "But then she always is."

Lou smiled. "Well, Grandpa said to tell you that everything will be ready in half an hour, Amy."

Amy felt her stomach contract at the thought of Thanksgiving dinner without Mom. "But there's these two to bring in and the stables to be skipped out," she gabbled, "and the feeds to do. There's no way I can be ready in half an hour. You know, maybe you and Grandpa better go ahead and eat without me..."

"Amy," Lou's voice interrupted her. Her cornflower-blue gaze was sympathetic but firm. "You know Grandpa's put a lot of effort into this dinner. We all have to eat it together –

that's the point. We'll give you a hand with the horses, won't we, Scott?"

"Sure." Scott nodded.

Amy's throat felt dry but she knew that Lou was right. "OK," she said, fighting to keep her voice steady. "If you can open the gate, I'll lead Melody in. Daybreak should follow."

However, when Amy led Melody out of the field, Daybreak stayed stubbornly where she was. Having tasted freedom for the first time, she now seemed reluctant to give it up. Melody whickered anxiously to her. Daybreak's eyes flickered from the field to her mother.

Scott went into the field. "Go on," he said encouragingly.

With a pert toss of her head, the filly put her ears back and cantered after Melody. Upon reaching the mare, she nipped her flank sharply as if to tell her off for leaving her.

"Hey!" Amy protested. Flattening her ears, Daybreak snaked her head at her but Amy simply laughed and pushed her away. "You are going to have to learn some manners, baby," she told the foal. Daybreak looked at her haughtily and Amy was reminded of Scott's earlier words. Daybreak was going to be a handful – no doubt about that.

After Melody and Daybreak had been settled in their stall in the back barn and the horses' straw beds had been tidied up, Scott left for his family's Thanksgiving meal. Amy watched from the stone-flagged feed-room as Lou walked down the yard with him. They stopped by his car and kissed. Lou watched until the vehicle disappeared out of sight and then came back up the yard, a dreamy smile playing at the corners of her mouth.

"What do you want me to do?" Lou asked as she entered the feed-room.

"Can you add some cod-liver oil to those and then mix them?" Amy said, pointing to a pile of feeds she had made up earlier.

Her sister nodded absent-mindedly. "OK." She looked out of the door again and then turned back to Amy, frowning. "What did you just say?"

"Lou!" Amy exclaimed. At twenty-three, Lou might be eight years older than her, but at that moment it felt like the other way round. Amy picked up the dusty cod-liver oil tin and put it into her sister's hands. "Cod-liver oil – in feeds – then mix." She grinned as she propelled her normally sensible sister towards her task.

Lou started to pour dollops of the oil into the horses' food. "Scott's invited me to a Christmas reunion dinner in three weeks' time," she said breathlessly. "It's for all the vets in his year at college. It's black tie, so I'll have to find something special to wear. Will you come shopping with me next week?"

"Sure," Amy said, starting to stir the feeds. She could never be bothered to go clothes shopping for herself, but helping Lou buy a gorgeous dress might be fun.

"I was thinking, you and Matt should get together," Lou said. "Then we could all go out on a date."

"Well, it's not going to happen," Amy said, thinking of Scott's younger brother, Matt. He was one of her best friends and he'd been trying to persuade her to go out with him for ages.

"Why not?" Lou said. "Scott says Matt really likes you."

"Yeah, and I like him," Amy said. "But *not* like that."

"So who do you like?" Lou said.

Amy shrugged and started to pile the feeds up. "No one." It was the truth. There wasn't anyone at school that she wanted to date. *And probably just as well*, she thought. With winter setting in, there was always so much to do on the yard. She was up at six o'clock every morning and hardly ever stopped before midnight. The only boys she ever saw outside school hours were Heartland's two stable-hands, Ty and Ben. For a moment an image of quiet, dark-haired Ty rose in her mind and she blushed, remembering a day way back in the summer when he had touched her cheek and a shock like fire had run through her veins.

Lou obviously saw the blush. "Amy?" she said in delight. "There *is* someone, isn't there? Who is it?"

"There isn't anyone," Amy said quickly, pushing Ty out of her mind. She was being dumb. Ty was like a brother and best friend to her, not a boyfriend. "There really isn't." She grabbed the pile of feeds. "I'll go and give these out," she said, hastily leaving the feed-room before Lou could question her any more.

* * *

The two sisters were rinsing the buckets by the water tap when the back door of the farmhouse opened and the tall figure of Jack Bartlett appeared. "Almost finished?" he called. Suddenly his upright shoulders bowed and he coughed heavily.

Amy frowned. She'd heard him coughing during the night, too. "Are you OK, Grandpa?"

Jack cleared his throat. "It's just a bad cold," he said, nodding. "I guess I picked it up the other night when we were foaling Daybreak." He changed the subject. "Now, are you coming in? Dinner's ready."

"We're coming," Lou replied.

As Grandpa turned back into the house, Lou gently took the water bucket from Amy. "Come on, Amy," she said. "It's time to eat."

Amy took a deep breath and followed Lou down to the back door. *It's going to be all right*, she told herself. She looked at Lou. Her sister appeared so composed; it was almost as though she didn't care that this was their first Thanksgiving since Mom had died. But Amy knew her sister better than that. Lou cared *just* as deeply as she did. It was just that she had a different way of coping, channelling her energy into being practical and sensible.

At the porch, Amy pulled off her boots as Lou opened the door into the warm, brightly lit and cluttered kitchen. Grandpa was lifting a perfectly golden roast turkey out of the oven.

"It all smells delicious, Grandpa," Lou said, going over to the sink to wash her hands. "Can I do anything to help?"

Amy stopped in the doorway, her heart pounding. Everything looked so familiar — the red and white candles on the table, the huge pumpkin pie cooling on the dresser, the dishes of home-made cranberry sauce, sweet potatoes and chestnut stuffing. As her eyes fell on the place settings, she let out a strangled sob. At the far end of the table, where Mom had always sat, the tablecloth was bare.

Lou and Grandpa swung round at the sound of her crying.

Grandpa, his face creasing in concern, put down the turkey and hurried over.

As his arms folded round her, Amy felt the grief that she'd been controlling so well over the last few months overwhelm her. She remembered so clearly the day when she had persuaded her mom to take the trailer out on to lonely Clairdale Ridge to rescue Spartan, a half-starved stallion. She also remembered the storm and the tree falling, then the waking up in hospital with Lou telling her the news. Mom was dead.

She didn't know how long she cried for, but at last she became aware of the room again and of the rough wool of her grandpa's jumper prickling her face. "I'm sorry," she muttered, pulling back and trying to regain some control over her feelings.

"It's OK, honey — it's natural," her grandpa said. "Times like these are never easy when we've lost someone we love."

Amy looked into his blue eyes and saw the understanding there. "I miss her, Grandpa. So much…" she whispered, her heart clenching with loss. "And it's not just today, it's every day…"

Grandpa kissed her hair. "We all miss your mom. We always will. But we've got each other, and today of all days we need to give thanks for that. It's what your mom would have wanted. You know how much she believed in looking forward to the future, not back at the past."

Lou rubbed Amy's arm. "Grandpa's right, Amy."

Amy swallowed and nodded.

"Come on," Grandpa said, hugging her one more time. "Let's eat."

The atmosphere around the table was subdued as they sat down. "I wonder what Daddy's doing right now?" Lou said, breaking the silence as they began to hand round the hot vegetable dishes.

Amy glanced quickly at Grandpa. His face had tightened. "Probably nothing special," she said quickly. "They don't have Thanksgiving in England, do they?"

"No," Lou admitted. "But he might be thinking of us."

"I'm sure he is, sweetheart," Grandpa said, only his taut mouth betraying his feelings. Amy knew Grandpa had never forgiven Tim, their father, for abandoning them and their mom after a riding accident had ended his international showjumping career twelve years ago.

"I hope he got my last letter," Lou said, referring to the

one she had posted a week ago. "I asked him to ring us today."

"Well, maybe he will," Grandpa said.

Seeing the pain in his eyes, Amy jumped to her feet. "We haven't said thank you for the horses," she said, blurting out the first thing she could think of to change the subject. "Mom always used to – we should too."

Grandpa nodded. "You're right." He stood up and took down a thick, dusty photograph album from the top shelf of the dresser. He offered it to Amy. "Would you like to?"

Amy hesitated for a moment. She hadn't really thought beyond the need to divert the conversation from Daddy. "Oh," she said slowly. She took the heavy leather book and opened it, swallowing a lump in her throat. Page after page was filled with photographs of horses that had been treated at Heartland. Amy looked inside the front cover and saw her mom's familiar writing: *By healing, we heal ourselves.*

"If you don't want to…" Grandpa began, looking at her face in concern.

"No," Amy said. "I want to." And suddenly she meant it. "Mom often told me how privileged she was, being able to work with the horses. Well, I feel the same," Amy said, thinking of all the horses *she* had helped in the five months since her mom had died – Sugarfoot, Spartan, Promise, Melody … the list went on. "Every Thanksgiving, Mom said that by healing, we heal ourselves, and it's true. The horses I've helped have given me so much and so I'd like to give thanks to them, just like Mom would have done."

Grandpa lifted his glass. "To the horses," he said. "To those in the past, in the present, and to those still to come."

"To the horses," Amy and Lou echoed quietly.

They put their glasses down and picked up their knives and forks. Amy glanced across at Lou. She was looking at the photograph album, her eyes shadowed. "I wish I could have been here to hear Mom say those words," she said sadly.

Grandpa looked at her sympathetically. "You were always working, Lou."

"Yes," Lou said slowly. "I suppose I was."

When they had finally finished eating the pumpkin pie, Amy and Lou cleared away the dishes and plates and then they all settled down for the evening in front of the TV. Around ten o'clock, Amy glanced at her watch. "I'd better go and check on the horses," she said, standing up.

Grandpa stood up too and started to cough. "Do you want a hand?"

Before Amy could reply, Lou jumped to her feet. "You don't sound too good, Grandpa. You stay here in the warm – I'll help."

After pulling on their jackets and boots, the girls went outside into the frosty night air. Lou seemed unusually subdued as they went around the stalls, collecting the empty hay nets and checking the water buckets and rugs. Amy looked at her sister and wondered what was on her mind.

When they'd finished, Lou went over to Sugarfoot's stall

and with a sigh leant against the half-door. "I wish I'd been here for at least one Thanksgiving with Mom."

Amy felt awkward. "You were always too busy to come to Heartland, Lou."

"I could have come," Lou said. "I didn't really have to work every holiday."

"Mom understood how you felt," Amy told her. "She knew that the horses reminded you too much of Daddy and that staying away was easier."

"Even so, I should have come." Lou stretched out her hand to stroke the little Shetland. "I should have made the effort. I didn't and now..." She swallowed and looked down. "Now, it's too late."

Amy squeezed her arm.

Lou turned. "I missed out on building a real friendship with one parent; I'm not going to make the same mistake again."

Unease stirred through Amy. "What do you mean?"

"Daddy," Lou said. "I can't stop thinking about him. I'm going to find him, Amy. I don't care what I have to do."

Chapter Two

That night, Amy lay in bed thinking about Lou's words. She had been just three years old when Daddy had left and she had no real memories of him, just the odd photo her mom had kept of him riding his horse, Pegasus. After the accident, she and her mom had left England to live with Grandpa in Virginia, while Lou, convinced that Daddy would one day return, had begged to stay on at her English boarding school. Their mom was reluctant to cause Lou any more emotional stress, so she had agreed. On her rare visits to Heartland, Lou made no secret of the fact that she thought Mom and Amy had been wrong to leave England.

Shortly after their mom's death, Amy and Lou had discovered a letter, sent by their father to their mom five years before, begging for a reconciliation. Marion had never replied, but Lou was determined to find their father and had written to the address on the letterhead asking to meet up.

Amy hugged her knees to her chest and tried to imagine seeing her father. Three weeks ago, she had caught a fleeting glimpse of him at Mom's grave, but she hadn't realized who he was. It was only later that Grandpa admitted that Tim had visited Heartland earlier that day, and that he had sent him packing. For a while, Amy had thought that Lou was never going to forgive Grandpa — but, eventually, on the night of Daybreak's birth, the two of them had made their peace.

Amy sighed. What would happen if Daddy *did* come back into their lives? After her mom's death, everything had been turned upside-down — Lou had come back from her big job in Manhattan and Ty and Amy had learnt how to treat the horses on their own. It had been a time of upheaval and change but, at last, life had begun to settle down. If Daddy made contact again, surely there would just be more changes to cope with.

Amy shut her eyes. It felt as if a distant storm-cloud was looming ominously on the horizon. With a shiver, she tried to blank the thought out of her mind.

Amy woke up early the next morning. The air was still and frosty when she took her pony, Sundance, for an early-morning ride.

When she returned, forty minutes later, Amy heard the familiar noisy rattle of Ty's pick-up coming up the drive. She put Sundance away in his stall and strode down the yard to greet him.

"Hi," she called. "Did you have a good Thanksgiving?"

"Yeah, pretty cool," Ty called back, slamming the truck's door shut and pushing back his dark hair from his eyes. Slim but muscular, he stood only a few inches taller than Amy. "But what about you? I guess it must have been tough."

Amy shrugged. Having worked at Heartland for the last two and a half years, Ty knew her so well that it was pointless for her to pretend otherwise. "It wasn't easy," she admitted, "but I got through it." Not wanting to dwell on the day before, she changed the subject. "I turned Daybreak and Melody out in the afternoon."

To her relief, Ty didn't make any comment on her swift change of subject. "How were they?"

As they walked up to the tack-room, Amy filled him in. "Daybreak's finding her independence," she said. "I think the sooner we teach her to lead, the better. She doesn't seem to feel the need to be close to her mother much."

Ty nodded. "We'll start today."

"This morning," Amy said. "I'm meeting Matt at the shops this afternoon."

Ty raised his eyebrows. "Oh yeah, you and Matt out on a date, hey?"

"No way!" Amy exclaimed. "For your information, Soraya's going to be there too. We're *all* going Christmas shopping together." She shook her head. "Honestly!" she exclaimed. "What's wrong with everyone here? Matt's just a friend — that's all!"

After the horses had been fed and the stalls cleaned out, Amy and Ty went up to Melody and Daybreak's stall. The aim was to teach Daybreak to walk up to the field on a lead-rope instead of letting her just run loose, as she had done the day before.

Amy knew it was vital that Daybreak learnt to be led. Her mom had always said that learning to accept the restraint of a halter and lead-rope was the most important lesson any young horse could ever be taught. But she had been totally against any sort of physical domination, believing instead that a horse should learn to submit willingly to the handler. *Force destroys trust*, she had always said, *and without trust, there can never be a true partnership*.

Amy remembered these words as she walked up to Daybreak and Melody's stall. She had been handling the little filly regularly to try and gain her trust. Although Daybreak had at first resisted her, Amy had persisted and now she would stand while Amy ran her hands over her head, legs and body. Admittedly she didn't seem to enjoy it, but she accepted it and that was the main thing.

The plan was for Ty to lead Melody out to the field, while Amy followed behind with Daybreak on a halter and lead-rope. The lead-rope was not going to be used to pull or force the foal — simply to guide her in the right direction. If Daybreak stopped, then Amy was going to encourage her to move forwards by placing an arm around the foal's hindquarters and applying gentle forward pressure. Amy had seen her mom do it many times and felt confident that they wouldn't have any problems.

As Ty opened the stall door, Melody whinnied a greeting. "Hi, girl," Amy said. Daybreak was standing behind her mother. Amy clicked her tongue but the little foal just looked arrogantly at her and didn't move.

"We'd better just thread the lead-rope through the back of Daybreak's halter, rather than snapping the hook on to the metal ring," Ty said, starting to put on Melody's halter. "Then, if the worst happens and she *does* get loose, the end of the rope will just slip out through the leather. We don't want to risk her running round the yard with the rope still attached to her halter."

Amy nodded. It was a sensible precaution. She approached Daybreak, who presented her hindquarters to Amy and lifted one back leg warningly. "Come here," Amy said, neatly side-stepping the filly's quarters and closing in on her head. Almost before Daybreak knew what was happening, Amy had got the halter over her nose and was slipping the end of the rope through the back.

Daybreak tossed her head but Amy kept hold of her. "Don't be silly," she said. "It's going to be OK."

Ty led Melody out of the stall. At first, all went well. Daybreak realized that she was going to the field and followed her mother eagerly. Amy simply held the lead-rope loosely and walked alongside her. Then, halfway up the yard, Daybreak suddenly stopped.

"Walk on," Amy encouraged, putting her right hand around the filly's quarters and pressing lightly. Whenever she had seen her mom apply the same method, the foal had always walked forward. Not Daybreak: throwing her head high, she dug her heels in. Amy increased the pressure. "Walk on," she said more firmly.

With a speed that took Amy completely by surprise, Daybreak shot backwards. She reached the end of the lead-rope before Amy could release it from her hand. As the rope tightened and stopped her with a jerk, Daybreak gave an enraged squeal and rose on her back legs, her head fighting against the restraint, her front legs striking the air.

"Let go of the rope!" Ty shouted, looking round and seeing what was going on. "She'll go over, Amy!"

But Amy had seen the danger the foal was in and, acting instinctively, had already loosened the rope. The end of it slithered through the halter and Daybreak was free. As her front hooves landed lightly on the yard, she plunged side-ways and came to a trembling halt.

"Easy, Melody, easy," Ty said, trying to calm the mare, who was struggling to get to her foal. "What happened?" he demanded as he brought Melody under control.

"I put my arm behind her and she just went crazy," Amy exclaimed, staring at the foal. Her heart was pounding as she thought about how close Daybreak had come to injuring herself. Amy stepped towards the foal to try and catch her again but she shied away.

"Leave her," Ty said quickly. "She needs a chance to calm down. Let's just put them out in the field."

"But if we do that, she'll think that by fighting the rope she gets her own way," Amy protested.

"I know, but look how tense she is," Ty replied. "If we try to do anything with her now, she's just going to resist us all the more."

Amy hesitated. It was a dilemma. If they gave in to Daybreak now then she would have learnt a damaging lesson, but Ty was right – they didn't want to get into a fight with her. Nodding her head, she reluctantly agreed and went ahead of Ty to open the field gate.

Ty led Melody into the field and set her free. Keeping a wary eye on Amy, Daybreak shot through the gate and up to her mother. The filly stopped dead, shoved her head against Melody's belly and began to feed. She didn't look at all upset by her recent experience. In fact, there was an almost cheeky wag to her tail as she suckled.

Amy felt awful. This was the first proper lesson in leading and it had ended disastrously. "What did I do wrong?" she said. "I never saw a foal act like that with Mom. Did I scare her or something?"

"Scare her?" Ty echoed in astonishment. "No way. You saw her. She wasn't scared of that rope, she was fighting it."

"But why?" Amy said.

"She's a very dominant filly," Ty said. "You can see it in her eyes. Most horses are naturally submissive. In the wild, they

do as the lead-stallion or mare demands. When we train them, they learn to submit to us in the same way. Most horses are fine with that. But just occasionally you'll get one who isn't — the type of horse who would have *been* a lead-stallion or mare in the wild. They'll fight against any form of restraint." He looked at Daybreak. "They used to be called rogue horses."

"But Mom always said that there's no such thing!" Amy burst out. "Horses aren't born bad, it's people that make them turn bad."

"I know," Ty said quickly. "And of course I agree that that's true in nearly all cases. But that doesn't change the fact that a few horses are born with the instinct to fight control, not submit to it — Daybreak's one of those and that's going to make her difficult to train."

"She'll learn," Amy protested. "She's only a baby."

Ty didn't say anything for a moment. "Yeah," he said at last. "You're right. She's young and, providing we're patient, she'll learn." He fastened the gate. "But I don't think we should try leading her on the yard again just yet — at least not until we've done a whole load more handling."

Amy nodded. He was right. Until Daybreak accepted pressure being applied to move her forwards, it was far too dangerous to try and lead her around. She looked at the fiery little filly in the field. It looked like training her to be led was going to be far more difficult than she'd imagined.

Lou dropped Amy off in town just after two o'clock. Lights

glittered on every tree and shopfront and carols boomed out through loudspeakers as she made her way through the crowds. Just about everyone seemed to be out shopping. At last, she caught sight of Matt and Soraya waiting by Huckleberries Ice-Cream Parlour.

"Hi!" she gasped as she reached them. "Sorry I'm late. I just got busy with the lunchtime feeds and turning out and..."

Matt grinned. "Yeah, yeah – and anyway, why change the habit of a lifetime?"

"I'm not *always* late," Amy protested.

"Only ninety-nine point nine per cent of the time," Soraya teased. "So, what shopping have you got to get?"

"Everything," Amy said, as they started to make their way through the crowds. "All my Christmas gifts – *and* it's Ty's birthday soon. I've got to get something for that."

"Hang on, I need to find a belt for Scott," Matt said, dashing into a leather store they were just passing.

Soraya looked at the display of belts, wallets and coats in the window. "Maybe I should get something for Ben," she said. "What do you think?"

"I don't know," Amy said. It was a tough question to answer. She knew Soraya liked Ben, but although he seemed to get on well with her, he hadn't shown any sign of asking her out. "I mean, you don't want to get him a present if he only gives you a card."

"I know," Soraya said. "But what if he does get me something and I haven't got him anything?"

They frowned at each other, considering the difficult dilemma. "I know. I'll try and find out whether he's planning on getting you something," Amy said.

Just then, Matt came back out of the shop with a small parcel in his hand. "That's my first gift bought," he said with some satisfaction. He dug a list out of the pocket of his jeans.

"You're so organized," Amy said, as they set off through the crowd again. "How do you know what to get everyone?" Her own shopping was much more haphazard. She tended to buy things on impulse, not having any clear plans but just waiting until she saw something she liked.

"I just asked everyone before I came out. That way it makes my life a lot easier," Matt grinned, as Amy began to think that she should have been a bit more practical.

"But you didn't ask me what *I* wanted," she teased.

"Me neither," joined in Soraya.

"Er ... well, it's a surprise," Matt started. "Now, I could go to that shop that sells aromatherapy stuff," he said consulting his piece of paper. "I want to get something for Mom. You know about aromatherapy, Amy. I need a bit of help here."

"I thought you'd made a list," Soraya exclaimed.

"I did, but ... er ... Scott was the only one around when I made it," Matt admitted. "I'm guessing the rest."

"So much for making your life easier," Amy laughed. "Come on, then, let's go." She began to think what *she* might buy at the aromatherapy shop – some oils for Lou, maybe something for Ty? Suddenly her eyes fell on a group of three girls approaching from the opposite direction. "Oh, great!" Amy groaned to Soraya. "Look who it is."

Ashley Grant and her two friends, Jade Saunders and Brittany Phillips, were sauntering through the crowd, looking immaculate in their designer clothes. Ashley Grant was Amy's least-favourite person in the world. Her family owned a highly successful hunter-jumper training stable called Green Briar. It was close to Heartland, but the methods they used there could not have been more different. Val Grant, Ashley's mom and the head trainer at Green Briar, believed in using force and firm discipline.

"Come on, let's go," Soraya said, grabbing Amy's arm. She didn't like Ashley and her bitchy friends any more than Amy did.

"Is Dan still dating Brittany?" Amy asked Matt as they followed Soraya. Dan Evans was Matt's friend from the football team.

"Yeah," Matt replied. "They've been seeing each other quite a bit. We all went to a movie on Wednesday night – Ashley came too."

Amy raised her eyebrows sarcastically. "That must have been fun."

Matt smiled. "She's not that bad when you get to know her."

Amy stared at him in disbelief. "This *is* Ashley Grant we're talking about, isn't it?"

"She's sent me an invitation to her Christmas party," Matt said.

This piece of information was enough to stop Soraya and Amy in their tracks. "What? *You're* going to the Grants' Christmas party?" Soraya exclaimed.

"Hey, not just me," Matt said hastily, seeing the expression on their faces. "There's a whole load of guys from the football team going."

Amy could hardly believe it. Every year, the Grant family held a huge Christmas party at their very large house. Ashley talked about it for weeks in advance and afterwards; people at school who cared about that sort of thing considered it *the* party to be invited to. However, the invitations were very exclusive and even Matt, who was very popular, had never been invited before. "And you're going to go?" she said incredulously.

"Sure," Matt shrugged. "Why not?"

"Amy! Wait up!"

Amy swung round. It was Ashley. She was pushing her way through the crowds, waving.

Amy's muscles tensed. Ashley only ever spoke to her to make sarcastic comments – usually about Heartland. However, there was no way Amy was going to run away. Lifting her chin, she held her ground. "Hello, Ashley," she said coolly as Ashley reached her. She waited for the cutting remark but, to her surprise, Ashley's lips, perfectly defined by rose-red lipstick, curved into a smile.

"Hi there," she said. "How are you?"

Amy stared at her in astonishment. Ashley Grant had just asked her how she was and, even weirder, sounded like she *meant* it. She looked at Soraya and saw that her friend's brown eyes were wide with incredulity.

Hardly noticing that Amy hadn't replied, Ashley carried on. "Did you have a good Thanksgiving?" She paused for a fraction of a second. "It must have been busy with all the horses you have at the moment. Were Ty and Ben around to help?"

Having expected a fight, Amy could hardly get her head round this new-style Ashley. Feeling like she was in some sort of crazy dream, she shook her head. "They both had the day off."

"Are they going to be away for the whole weekend?" Ashley asked.

"No, Ty's back today and Ben's back tomorrow," Amy said.

"Oh, that's good," Ashley said. She looked up at Matt with her cat-like green eyes. "Now, did you get my invitation for the party, Matt?"

"Yeah," Matt replied. "Thanks."

Ashley turned back to Amy. "You must come as well, Amy," she gushed.

"You're inviting *me* to your party?" Amy said in astonishment.

"Of course." Ashley said this as though it were the most natural thing in the world for her to invite Amy. Suddenly she seemed to remember Soraya. "You too, Soraya," she added. "I'll drop your invitation off with Amy's tomorrow."

Amy frowned. The last thing she wanted was to go to the Grants' stuck-up party. "It's OK..." she began, about to tell Ashley not to bother, but Ashley interrupted her.

"Sorry, Amy," she said, smiling widely. "I'd really love to stay and talk but I must run. I'll see you tomorrow!" And with that, she turned and flounced away to where Jade and Brittany were waiting.

For a moment, Amy and Soraya stared after her in stunned silence.

"Did I just dream that?" Soraya said in a strangled voice. "Or did Ashley really just come over here and invite us to her party?"

"It *has* to be a dream," Amy said.

"Or else there's something totally weird going on," Soraya said. "Like aliens have come and taken over Ashley's body."

"Come on, you guys," Matt protested. "I told you – Ashley's not that bad. It's Thanksgiving. She must have remembered about your mom, Amy. Maybe she was just trying to be friendly."

Amy and Soraya looked at each other. At the same moment they shook their heads. "No – aliens," they said together.

Soraya grinned at Amy. "So, are we going to go?"

"No way," Amy said. She caught a look of disappointment cross Soraya's face and she frowned in surprise. "Why? You don't want to, do you?"

Soraya hesitated. "Well, it could be kind of fun, but I won't go if you don't," she added hastily.

"Yeah, come!" Matt urged. "I'll have a way better time if you two are there."

Amy frowned. She didn't really want to go but Matt and Soraya both looked so keen. "Let's see if Ashley brings the invitations round first," she said sceptically.

Much to Amy's surprise, Ashley turned up at Heartland the next morning. It wasn't ideal timing. Having decided to try and handle Daybreak once more before attempting to use the lead-rope again, Ty was holding the foal in the field while Amy was running her hands over her body, legs and head.

Daybreak had stood reasonably still for five minutes. However, at exactly the moment that the Grants' silver Mercedes drew into the yard, Amy decided to try and persuade Daybreak to move forward a step. The second the little filly felt Amy's left arm pressing around her hindquarters, she shot violently backwards in protest. Amy jumped back just in time to avoid being trampled and Ty only just managed to hang on to Daybreak.

"Looks like you've got a difficult one there!"

"Oh no," Amy groaned to Ty as she looked round and saw the figure of Val Grant striding towards the gate.

Ashley followed her mom. Her expensive black breeches clung to her legs and her pale-blonde hair fell to her shoulders in a gleaming sheet. She looked like a glamorous model from a magazine advertising riding clothes. Amy suddenly felt very aware of the straw in her own hair and the stains all over her worn-out jeans.

"Causing you some problems, is she?" Val Grant said, nodding at Daybreak.

Amy gritted her teeth. "Nothing we can't manage," she said.

Val Grant ignored her words. "I wouldn't let a little thing like that mess me around," she said, her eyes narrowing as they swept over the defiant filly. "I'd tie one of her legs up and force her to the ground. Keep her there until she gives up fighting. You need to show her who's the boss right from the start."

Angry words leapt into Amy's mouth, but before she could say anything Ty stepped forward. "That's not how we do things here," he said levelly, only the darkening of his eyes revealing how angry *he* was too. "But thank you for your advice, Mrs Grant."

Val Grant's face hardened and, for a moment, tension crackled in the air. It was broken by Ashley producing an envelope from her pocket. "Here're the invitations for our party," she said, handing it to Amy. She'd been so busy looking round at the yard that she had hardly seemed to notice the exchange between her mom, Amy and Ty. "I bought one for you as well, Ty, and one for Ben. Do you think he might like to come, Amy?"

Amy was still seething with anger at Val Grant's comments. "Why don't you ask him yourself?" she snapped. "He's over there."

Ashley spun round. Ben was walking down the yard with a water bucket in his hand. "Ben!" Ashley called out, waving.

Ben looked round. He had only met Ashley once before and for a moment a frown creased his handsome face as he tried to place her. But then Amy saw a look of recognition dawn in his eyes. "Hi," he said, coming over. "It's Ashley, isn't it? You're one of Amy's friends."

Ashley flicked her long hair back and smiled up at him. "That's right," she said. "I met you at a show last weekend. This is my mom, Val. Mom, this is Ben Stillman."

"Pleased to meet you," Ben said, holding out his hand to Val Grant.

Val Grant looked at Ben with interest. "You're Lisa Stillman's nephew, aren't you? From the Fairfield Arabian Stud?"

"Yeah," Ben said. "My aunt sent me here to Heartland to learn about treating problem horses."

Val Grant snorted derisively. "Well, she can't be counting on you learning much."

Ben looked confused.

"We just called by to drop off some invitations for a family party we're having two weeks today," Ashley stepped in quickly. "There's one for you too. I thought, with you being new in the neighbourhood, you might like the chance to come along and meet some people." She fluttered her long eyelashes at him. "Oh ... you *will* come, won't you?"

"Sure," Ben said, looking pleased. "Thanks for asking me."

Ashley held his gaze. "It's my pleasure."

It was like a light had gone on in Amy's head. *That was it!* That was why Ashley was being so friendly — she liked Ben but she couldn't invite him to the party without asking everyone else too. Suddenly, it all made sense.

But what about Soraya? Amy glanced anxiously at Ben for a sign he was attracted to Ashley — but, to her relief, he was simply smiling in his usual easy way.

"Well, I guess I'd better get back to work," he said. He turned to Val Grant. "Nice to meet you, Mrs Grant."

"You too, Ben," Val Grant replied.

"See you," Ben said to Ashley and then, with a quick smile at Amy and Ty, he headed back to the water tap.

Ashley watched him go and then swung round. "Come on, Mom, let's go. See you at school, Amy," she added, almost curtly, as the Grants walked back to their Mercedes.

"OK," Ty said slowly, looking down incredulously at the invitation in his hand as Ashley and Val got into the car. "Have you got any idea what *that* was all about?"

"Yep." Amy explained her theory to him.

"Ashley likes Ben!" Ty repeated in astonishment.

"I'm sure of it," Amy replied. "That's the only reason she's invited us to the party. Did you see the way she was looking at him?" She dropped her voice in an imitation of Ashley's husky purr. "Oh, Ben, you really *must* come."

Ty grinned. "Poor Ben — do you think he has any idea what he's in for?"

"I don't know, but I'm going to find out," Amy said. She went down to the water butt where Ben was just turning off the tap. "Looks like you've got a fan," Amy said. Her voice was teasing but inside her heart was thumping. She hoped – desperately hoped – that he wasn't going to say he liked Ashley.

A look of surprise crossed Ben's face. "What do you mean?"

"Ashley Grant," Amy said. "Ben!" she exclaimed seeing his blank look. "You can't have missed the way she was flirting with you."

"Ashley?" Ben said incredulously. "That girl who was here just now?"

"Yeah, blonde, slim, looks like a model," Amy said.

Ben shrugged. "Yeah, well... She's not my type. I met loads of girls like that when I was living at my aunt's – rich, beautiful and nearly always boring."

Amy felt a rush of relief. "So you're not interested?" she asked casually.

Ben shook his head. "I'm not looking to get involved with anyone yet. There's enough going on in my life, what with Red and learning about things here and getting to know my mom again after all this time." He picked up the bucket. "This party sounds like fun, though. Are you, me and Ty all going to go together?"

Amy shook her head. She knew Soraya and Matt wanted her to go but she really didn't want to. "I don't think I'll go."

"Why not?" Ben said in surprise.

Amy shrugged. "It's not my sort of thing and I doubt it's Ty's either."

Ben looked dismayed. "But I only accepted the invitation because I thought you'd both be going. I don't want to go on my own."

Amy felt bad. It was mean to make Ben go by himself — he would hardly know anyone there. And besides, as much as she hated to admit it, there was a little part of her that was curious about the Grants' house and what their famous party might involve.

"Come on, Amy," Ben pleaded. "Don't do this to me. Say you'll come."

"All right," she said. "I'll come."

"You will?" Ben looked very relieved. "Thanks. I owe you one."

Amy returned to Ty, who was handling Daybreak's legs again. "Well, it looks like I'm going to the Grants' party after all," she sighed.

"How come?" Ty said in surprise.

"I can't let Ben go on his own," Amy explained. She looked at him. "Please come with us, Ty."

Ty shrugged. "It's not really my kind of thing but..." he hesitated. "Well, if you and Ben are going then maybe I'll come along too." He stroked Daybreak. "Now, are we ready to try again?"

Amy nodded and took up her position at the side of

the foal. "You're sure you don't want to try Val Grant's suggestion?" she teased.

Ty's eyes met hers. "Quite sure," he said, and they both smiled.

The training session with Daybreak didn't go well. Time after time, when they applied pressure behind her, the little filly either ran backwards or simply refused to move. Amy and Ty grew hotter and hotter and soon discarded their heavy winter jackets.

"We're not going to give in," Amy said through gritted teeth after fifteen minutes had passed. "She *is* going to go forwards."

Even Ty, whose patience was usually endless, was beginning to look frazzled. "Come on, girl," he encouraged, taking a deep breath and taking hold of the halter again.

Suddenly Daybreak took a tiny step forwards.

"Good girl!" Amy cried, immediately releasing the pressure she had been applying under the foal's tail.

"At last," Ty exclaimed.

Amy rewarded Daybreak by rubbing her head. Most horses loved being stroked but the little foal looked at Amy mutinously – not objecting to the caress but not looking as if she were particularly enjoying it either. Amy sighed. It would be nice if, just once, Daybreak showed her some affection.

"Let's make that it for today," Ty said, wiping his arm across his forehead.

As they released the foal, Daybreak shook her head, wheeled round and plunged away, every muscle in her body expressing defiance again now that she was free. Amy watched as she trotted off. She loved the inner fire that burnt so strongly within Daybreak. The challenge was to harness it, channel it, so that she worked with rather than against them. Picking up her jacket, Amy left Ty to shut the gate and walked down the yard, deep in thought.

"Amy!"

Amy looked up. Lou was getting out of her car, a bundle of post from the letterbox at the end of the driveway in her hand. Her eyes shone as she waved a pale-blue envelope at Amy.

"Amy! Quick! It's a letter from Daddy! Come and see what it says!"

Chapter Three

Amy stopped dead in her tracks. Having put the other post on to the roof of the car, Lou was tearing open the airmail letter, her face flushed with excitement. Amy suddenly felt sick. *A letter from their father*. She walked slowly towards her sister.

Lou's eager blue eyes were scanning over the page. "He says he's really sorry he didn't get to see us. And he wants to meet up..."

Amy peered at the unfamiliar handwriting. It was slightly slanted, the letters neat and precise.

"Oh," Lou said suddenly. "He says he wants to meet in February. He'll be over here on business then."

For one brief second, Amy found her mind catching on to the word business. *Business — what sort of business? What did Daddy do?* And then she registered the flatness in Lou's voice. "February?" she echoed. "But that's three months away."

Lou nodded and Amy saw that the excited glow in her sister's eyes had been replaced by a faded look of disappointment. "I guess he must be busy until then." She looked at the letter again. "There isn't even a telephone number, so I can't ring him to see if he can come sooner. There's just an address." She handed the letter to Amy.

Tim Fleming, Amy read, *Oak Farm, Willoughby, Gloucestershire, England*. She turned the letter over and skimmed the contents.

> *My dear Lou,*
> *Thank you so much for your letter. I so wanted to meet you and Amy when I came over but your grandfather told me to stay away. I can't blame him for that — I know he was only trying to protect you — but if you only knew how much I've wanted to see you, how often I've thought about you... My two girls. What are you like now? Who do you take after? I would dearly love to meet up with you both. Unfortunately, I can't return at the moment, but perhaps in February? I'll be in New York on business then so I could fly down and visit. I'm sorry it can't be sooner but things are a bit difficult right now — I'll explain when I see you. Till then, take care, give my love to Amy and remember that I think about you both every day.*
> *All my love,*
> *Daddy*

Amy had to struggle to compose her thoughts. *Give my love to Amy*. She re-read the words three times. It was as if an invisible thread were stretching across the world, linking her with the father she had never really known. But she didn't want his love. What right did he have to suggest that she did? He wrote as if he had just been away on holiday, not missing from her life for twelve long years. And there wasn't even a single mention of their mom.

She handed the letter back to Lou. "What are you going to do?"

"I don't know," Lou replied slowly.

"It's not that long till February," Amy said.

Lou stared down at the letter and didn't reply.

For the rest of the day, Amy tried not to think about the letter. She didn't want to think about meeting Daddy. She wanted to block the whole thing from her mind. That evening, she rang Soraya and told her all about Ashley's visit. "You should have seen the way she was all over Ben!"

"Oh, great," Soraya groaned. "Like I really stand a chance if Ashley's after him."

"But he's not interested in her," Amy told her. "I asked him." She wondered whether to tell Soraya Ben's comment about not wanting to get involved with anyone at the moment, but held back. There was no point depressing Soraya — and anyway, she reasoned, he might not really have meant it. She tried to remember what he'd said about

Ashley. "Ben said he's met girls like her before and that they're really boring."

"Oh, help!" Soraya exclaimed. "If Ashley's boring then what am I?"

"Interesting," Amy said.

"Interesting!" Soraya exclaimed. "That makes me sound like a total freak."

Amy grinned. "Stop worrying. You are *not* a freak! So, are you going to come over and get ready for the party? Ben's offered to give me and Ty a lift; I'm sure he can squeeze all of us in."

"Then definitely," Soraya said. "It would be way too scary to have to turn up on my own."

"Soraya! It's only the Grants' Christmas party," Amy said.

"Exactly," Soraya said with feeling. She changed the subject. "So, what have you been doing today *apart* from hanging out with Ashley?"

"Well, Lou got a letter from Daddy," Amy said. "He wants to come and see us in February."

"February!" Soraya replied. Amy could hear the surprise in her friend's voice. "But that's months away."

"I don't care," Amy said, her voice getting harder.

"Really?" Soraya said.

"Yes, really," Amy replied. "He can do what he likes, as far as I'm concerned. It's Lou who wants to see him, not me."

* * *

Later that evening, Amy thought about what she'd said. It was true. She didn't care what her father did. But from somewhere deep inside, a little voice niggled her – was it that she didn't care or that she didn't *want* to care? There was a whole load of difference between the two.

Heartland's stalls were all full, so the next two weeks raced past as Amy juggled her time between the horses, school and seeing her friends. But, as usual, every spare minute she had was spent working with Ty and Ben in the yard. She was also trying to avoid being alone with Lou, worried that the conversation might turn towards Daddy. However, to her relief, Lou made no attempt to seek her out to discuss the subject and when they were with Jack neither of them spoke about it in case it upset him. He wasn't looking too well – the cold he had picked up the night of Daybreak's birth seemed to be lingering on, and his cough was getting worse. Amy and Lou tried to persuade him to see a doctor but he kept putting it off.

With everything that was happening, Amy managed to push the letter to the back of her mind. Whenever thoughts of it crept back to disturb her, she forced herself to think about Daybreak instead. Despite Amy and Ty being patient and gentle, the little filly was still resisting their attempts to train her. Some days she would move forwards when Amy applied pressure to her hindquarters, but mostly she would simply decide not to and would fight them every step of the way. Amy was starting to get worried. With each day that passed, Daybreak was getting physically stronger and harder to manage.

"I just don't understand why she's still like this," she said to Ty on a Friday afternoon as they looked over Daybreak and Melody's stall door after yet another unsatisfactory training session with the foal. "We've done everything we should."

"I was reading one of your mom's old books this morning," Ty said. "Perhaps we should have handled her more in the first twenty-four hours after she was born."

Amy thought back to Daybreak's first day. "But we were letting her bond with Melody," she said, remembering how for that reason they had decided leave handling the little foal until the following day.

"I know," Ty said. "But this book suggested that, if you handle a foal as early as possible, it will bond with you as much as with its dam. It's called imprinting. However, you need to do it in the first twenty-four hours – after that it's too late."

"But I did sleep that first night in Melody's stall," Amy frowned. "And Mom never had a problem with the foals she handled – and they weren't born here, they were sometimes two or three months old when she started working with them."

"But none of them were as naturally dominant as Daybreak," Ty said. "I'm not saying that we can't train her, only that it might have been a whole lot easier if we'd tried to get her to imprint from birth."

Amy looked at the little filly. She was lying down in the straw, her muzzle resting on one of her slender front legs, her hind legs curled up beneath her. Her dark eyes regarded them – fearless, intelligent and confident. Amy turned to Ty. "So, what can we do?"

"Well, I guess we've just got to be patient," Ty replied. "But it might also help if we try using some essential oils to calm her and make her more manageable. Vetiver oil is relaxing and balancing and good for horses that are headstrong."

Amy nodded. At Heartland, they often used aroma-therapy, herbs and Bach Flower Remedies to help deal with any horse's behavioural or emotional problems. "I'll get some vetiver from the tack-room," she said.

"OK," Ty said. "If you see to that, I'll finish off grooming Jasmine and Dancer."

Amy went down the frosty yard to the tack-room, where the essential oils were kept in the medicine cupboard. She took out a bottle of vetiver oil, a bottle of jojoba oil and an empty bottle, then decanted thirty millilitres of the jojoba into the empty bottle and added to it twelve drops of the vetiver. It was very important to dilute oils like vetiver with a base oil like jojoba, to prevent them from irritating the horse's skin. She'd just finished when Ben came into the tack-room carrying a grooming kit.

"What are you doing?" he asked, looking at the bottles with interest.

Amy was keen to get back to Daybreak and so she replied briefly. "Just working on something for Daybreak."

She was about to leave the tack-room when she caught sight of Ben's face. He was frowning. Amy felt a pang of guilt – he was working at Heartland so he could learn about the techniques that they used. She and Ty were so used to working together that they often forgot to explain the treatments to him.

"Do you want to come and see what I'm going to do?" she asked him.

"Sure," Ben said. He dumped the grooming bucket in the chest and joined her.

As they walked past the old stable block, Amy saw a ladder leaning against the wall. Grandpa was standing near the top, replacing some missing tiles on the roof. He was coughing hard and wheezing quite badly.

Amy stopped in concern. "Are you OK, Grandpa?" she asked when his coughing fit had subsided.

Jack looked round and attempted a smile. "I'm just fine," he said, his blue eyes watering. But he suddenly started to cough again, his hand reaching for his chest as if he were in pain.

Amy felt concerned. "You don't sound fine at all. You must make that doctor's appointment. Look, why don't you leave the roof till you're feeling a bit better?"

"This needs to be finished before the weather gets really bad," Jack said, determinedly picking up another tile. "Then I'll go in and phone."

"All right, but you must promise me that you will," Amy sighed. Knowing that when her grandpa had decided to do something it was useless to try and dissuade him, Amy reluctantly gave up.

"He's been up there all afternoon," Ben told her as they walked out of Jack's earshot.

They reached the warmth of the barn and Amy unbolted the stall door. Daybreak was still lying down. She lifted her head and stared at Amy with wary eyes. "First I've got to see her reaction to the prepared oil," Amy explained to Ben. "If she shows me that she likes it then I'll massage a little into her muzzle or poll."

"If she likes it?" Ben echoed. "What do you mean?"

"Watch," Amy said. As she went towards the little foal, Daybreak scrambled to her feet. "Steady," Amy soothed quickly grabbing the little foal's mane before she could swing her haunches round. So that she had some control of the foal, Amy captured Daybreak's nose with her free hand. Then she unscrewed the lid and offered the bottle to the filly for her to smell it. At first Daybreak threw her head back in rebellion at being held, but then the fragrant scent of the oil reached her nostrils. Blowing out in surprise, she seemed to forget about fighting Amy and lowered her muzzle close to the bottle. Amy held the bottle tightly in case Daybreak suddenly decided out of curiosity to nibble it, but she didn't. She sniffed the oil with each nostril in turn, then lifted her head and rolled her top lip back, showing her teeth.

"She likes it," Amy said, pleased.

"How do you know?" Ben asked.

"If she didn't then she'd just have sniffed it once or she'd have turned away and put her ears back," Amy said. "It's useless trying to treat a horse with anything they instinctively don't like. Somehow they seem to know which oils will help them and which won't. You have to listen to the horse and trust them to guide you."

"So what do you do now?" Ben asked curiously as Daybreak lowered her head to sniff the oil again.

Amy poured a little of the diluted oil into the palm of one hand and then handed Ben the bottle to look after. "Now I massage her with it," she said, catching hold of Daybreak's nose again and beginning to work the oil into the skin just between the filly's ears. "It might not work immediately, but hopefully there'll be a gradual change in her over the next few days. If nothing happens after a week then we have to try something else." Turning her attention to Daybreak, she focused on massaging in the oil. Letting her hands sense where to move, Amy concentrated on matching her breathing to the rhythm of her fingers. For once, the foal stood calmly, her delicate nostrils trembling as she breathed in and out. Enjoying this unfamiliar moment of peace between them, Amy began to feel a flicker of hope – maybe the oil would prove to be the solution to Daybreak's problems.

"There," Amy said at last, when the oil was completely

massaged in. "I'll do that twice a day for the next week. If there's no change after that, then we'll try something different."

As she left the stall, Ben looked puzzled. "But how does it actually work?" he said.

"Well, no one knows for sure," Amy said. "But it's thought that, as the chemicals in the oil are inhaled and absorbed through the skin into the bloodstream, they reach the emotional centre of the brain where they affect mood and attitude." She saw the slightly sceptical look in Ben's eyes. "As Mom always said — as long as it works, it doesn't matter how it happens." She bolted the stall door and took the bottle from Ben. "Come on, let's get started on the hay nets."

Amy woke early the next morning. As soon as she was dressed, she went to see Melody and her foal. Melody whickered when she saw her, and came over to nuzzle at Amy's hands. Amy rubbed her head and looked at Daybreak, who was standing in the back of the stall. Amy held out a hand. "Hi, girl."

With a squeal, Daybreak swung round and bucked, her tiny ears flat against her head. Amy sighed. It didn't look like the vetiver oil was working just yet.

After she had fed the horses, she went back down to the house to grab some breakfast. To her surprise, the table was set and Lou was bustling around the kitchen, cooking breakfast. "I've made some waffles," she said brightly as Amy came in. "Sit down. There's maple syrup and bacon on the table and some fresh coffee in the pot."

Amy stopped and stared. "You've made *waffles*?" she said. Usually the only person in the house to cook breakfast was Grandpa. If Lou got breakfast ready, there was never anything more than a bowl of cereal and a slice of toast.

"Yes, I thought I'd cook for us all," Lou said. "I've told Grandpa to lie in for a while – I heard him coughing really badly last night."

"Again?" Amy looked worried. "I told him he had to book an appointment at the doctor's."

"Yeah, and he has," Lou said. "Only he can't get an appointment for three days." She busied herself around the kitchen. "Now, sit down. Are waffles OK? Or would you prefer some scrambled eggs? I can whisk some up in no time."

"OK," Amy said, crossing her arms. "What's going on, Lou?"

"I don't know what you mean," Lou said. "I just thought it might be nice if I organized breakfast for a change."

Amy raised her eyebrows. "But all *this*?" She pointed at the table piled high with food.

Lou hesitated, then her shoulders suddenly sagged. "Well… You're right," she admitted, sinking down on to a chair. "There *is* a reason." She looked at the tablecloth. "I've … I've got something to tell you."

From the tone of her sister's voice, Amy could tell that she wasn't going to like what she had to say. "What is it, Lou?"

Taking a deep breath, Lou lifted her eyes. "I've made a decision, Amy," she said resolutely. "I'm going to England. I have to find Daddy."

Chapter Four

Amy stared at her sister, her heart thudding. "What do you mean?"

"I've booked a flight to London on Wednesday," Lou's eyes begged her to understand. "I know Daddy said he's coming over in February, but I can't wait till then. Thanksgiving made me realize that life's too short for family rifts. I need to see him now."

"But it's only two weeks till Christmas," Amy stammered, hardly able to take in what Lou was saying. "How long will you be away?"

"I'll be back before then," Lou said. "I've got his address so it won't take me long to find him."

"But can't you just ring him?" Amy said desperately. "Surely you can find out his phone number some way and speak to him on the phone. Why do you have to go and see him?"

"I tried to get the number but the operator said it wasn't listed," Lou replied. "Anyway, I don't just want to speak to him. I want to *see* him and get this all sorted out." She grasped the back of a chair. "I've been waiting for twelve years for this, Amy. Please say you understand."

For a moment, Amy battled with the desperate urge to beg Lou not to go. Part of her was terrified that her sister would never return. *Don't go, don't go*, she thought.

"Amy?" Lou said.

As much as Amy longed to plead with her to stay, she knew she couldn't. This was something Lou had to do. She took a deep breath. "I understand," she whispered, the words hurting her as she uttered them.

She was rewarded with a look of intense relief crossing Lou's face. She hugged Amy. "Thank you. It means a lot to me. I know it's hard at the moment, with Grandpa not being very well and…"

"I'm fine. What do you mean, I'm not well?"

Amy and Lou swung round. Jack was standing in the kitchen doorway looking pale and tired.

"Grandpa," Lou stammered. "How long have you been there?"

"I've just come down." A frown deepened on Jack's face as he looked from one grand-daughter to the other. "What's going on?"

Lou glanced nervously at Amy. "I think you better sit down, Grandpa." She told him what she'd just told Amy.

"I have to go, Grandpa," she said.

Amy looked anxiously at their grandpa's face. She knew how he felt about their father. How would he take the news?

For a moment, Jack didn't say anything. Then he squared his shoulders. "Lou," he said quietly. "I've always said that you should follow your heart — and if that's what it's telling you to do, then that's what you must do." He looked at Amy. "We'll cope, won't we, Amy?"

"I'm not going to leave you completely on your own," Lou said quickly. "I've rung my friend Marnie — you remember her, Grandpa? She stayed that time you were away at Glen and Silvia's. Well, she's got some time off and would love to come and stay again. She'll take over my work while I'm gone. She'd already mentioned coming to visit over the holidays — her parents are away in Fiji for Christmas and New Year, so when I asked her if she'd come and stay for longer she was really excited."

Amy was surprised but pleased. She liked Lou's friend Marnie a lot.

"What about Scott?" Grandpa asked. "Have you told him?"

"No, not yet. I only really decided yesterday that I was going to go, and I wanted to tell you both first," Lou replied. "He's coming round this morning, I'll tell him then."

Amy remembered something. "But you'll miss his reunion dinner."

"He'll understand," Lou said confidently. She smiled, looking as if a weight had been lifted from her shoulders now that she had told them. "I just can't wait to see Daddy again. Imagine his face when I just turn up at his door."

"Remember, you don't know anything about your father's life now," Grandpa said warningly. "Maybe you should write to him and let him know you're coming."

"There's no point," Lou said. "I'm flying on Wednesday, so I'll probably arrive before a letter could get to him anyway." She saw the concern on Grandpa's face. "Daddy wants to see me – his last letter made that clear."

"Yes, I know, but..." Grandpa broke off as Lou's face crumpled. "Look, just be careful, honey," he sighed, "that's all I'm saying."

Lou smiled. "I will." She hugged him. "You worry too much, Grandpa. Everything will be fine, you'll see."

After breakfast, Amy went out on to the yard. She walked up to Daybreak and Melody's stall and leant over the half-door, thinking hard about Lou's trip.

"Hi there." Amy turned round to see Ty coming down the aisle towards her. He frowned when he saw her face. "What's up?"

"It's Lou," Amy sighed. "She's going away." Miserably, Amy told Ty about Lou's plans. "What if she doesn't come back?" she said.

"She'll be back," Ty said reassuringly. "Her life's here now. You know she decided that when she gave up her job in New York."

"But what about Daddy? What if he wants her to stay with him?" Amy voiced her worst fears.

"Hey," Ty squeezed her shoulder. "Take it easy, Amy."

Amy took a deep breath and forced herself to stay calm.

"Come on," he said practically. "There's no point in standing round worrying about something that's just not going to happen. Let's go get started on those stalls."

At eleven o'clock, Scott drove up and parked outside the house. "Hi!" he called, jumping out as Amy came down the yard with a wheelbarrow. "Is Lou around?"

"She's in the house," Amy replied, for once hoping that he wouldn't come and talk to her.

He took a white envelope out of his pocket. "The tickets for the dinner arrived. Your sister's going to have to get a dress sorted out."

Just then, the front door opened and Lou came out. "Hi, Scott," she said quietly.

Scott bounded over to her. "Hi," he said, not seeming to notice her subdued manner. He kissed her enthusiastically. "Our tickets have arrived."

Lou glanced in Amy's direction.

Amy immediately took the hint. "I'd better go and turn Jasmine and Sundance out," she said, hastily dumping the wheelbarrow.

As she went up the yard, she heard Lou say, "Scott – we need to talk."

Out of earshot, Amy stopped and took a deep breath. She couldn't help wondering how Scott would take the news about Lou going away.

Ten minutes later, she heard his engine start up. She went cautiously back down the yard.

Lou was watching Scott drive away. Her face looked worried.

"How did it go?" Amy asked her tentatively.

Lou sighed and turned round. "It was all right — although he was a bit upset about the dinner," she said. "I don't think he really understood why I have to go to England right now." Lou paused for a moment. When she next spoke, her voice had a note of doubt in it for the first time. "I ... I am doing the right thing, aren't I, Amy?"

Amy struggled hard against her feelings. She knew Lou needed her support. "Of course you are," she said as convincingly as she could. "You heard what Grandpa said this morning. You've got to follow your heart, Lou."

Lou looked slightly happier. "Yes," she said. "You're right. That's what I'm going to do."

Soraya came round that afternoon and, as soon as the horses were fed, she and Amy went inside to get ready for the Grants' party. Amy had been saved the trouble of worrying about what to wear by the simple fact that she only had one dress that was suitable. It was a pale, shimmery, silvery colour and had tiny straps; sequins and beads were sewn round the hem of the floaty skirt that ended just above her knees. Lou had bought it for her from Bloomingdales a year ago, when Amy and Grandpa had been to stay with her in Manhattan. Amy had worn it that night in the city, but it had stayed in her wardrobe since then.

"I love that dress," Soraya said, as Amy took it out of its plastic wrap. "You should wear it more often."

Amy grinned. "Yeah, it would look really great when I was doing the mucking out." She shook the dress out. "What are you going to wear?"

Soraya took down two outfits from the back of Amy's door — a long black dress with a low back, and a short lilac shift-dress with tiny butterflies embroidered around the hem. "I couldn't decide. Which do you think?"

Amy looked from one to the other. "The lilac," she said decisively.

"But you haven't even thought about it," Soraya complained.

"I just like it best," Amy said. She couldn't see the point of agonizing about clothes for hours.

"But which do you think *Ben* would like?" Soraya asked.

"Both of them," Amy grinned, going over to her desk and putting a CD on. "Now, stop worrying and go and take a shower."

An hour later, they were just about ready. While Amy sprayed on some perfume borrowed from Lou, Soraya finished fixing the clips in her hair. Amy's party dress clung to her body and strappy silver shoes emphasized her slender ankles and calves. Her thick light-brown hair, blown dry for once, gleamed like silk, curling under just slightly at the ends. Usually when Amy went out she just wore a dash of mascara, but tonight Soraya had persuaded her to be more adventurous. She had used silver eyeshadow and eyeliner to highlight her grey eyes, and had finished off the look with a sweep of peachy blusher that gave a soft glow to her pale skin.

"You look great!" Soraya said as Amy looked critically at her reflection in the mirror.

"I just feel weird," Amy complained. "It doesn't look like me."

"You could always put your riding boots on underneath your dress," Soraya said teasingly.

"Don't tempt me!" Amy smiled.

Soraya put the final clip in place, and anxiously teased a few curls down around her face. "I love your hair like that," Amy told her. Then she glanced at her bedside clock and saw that it was nearly seven o'clock. "Come on, we'd better go downstairs!"

Grandpa and Lou were sitting together in the kitchen watching a TV game show. Grandpa was drinking a steaming hot mug of honey and lemon tea. They both looked up as Amy and Soraya entered.

"Wow! What a transformation!" Lou exclaimed.

Feeling very self-conscious, Amy hurried across the kitchen and grabbed her jacket.

"That's a gorgeous dress, Soraya," Lou said.

"Thanks," Soraya smiled.

"You both look perfectly beautiful," Jack said warmly, getting to his feet. As he did so, he coughed hard.

Amy looked at him in concern. "You sound awful, Grandpa."

"I'm all right," Grandpa said. "And if it doesn't get any better, I've got that doctor's appointment."

"All right, Grandpa," Lou said. "But promise you'll stay inside tomorrow."

"I'll see," Jack replied.

Just then, there was the sound of a truck drawing up outside the house. Grandpa looked out of the window as a horn hooted. "It looks like your lift is here. You girls enjoy yourselves."

"Yeah, have fun!" Lou said.

"We will," Amy replied. "See you later."

Ben and Ty were standing by the pick-up. Ben gave an appreciative whistle as he saw them. "Hey, look at the two of you!"

"You like?" Soraya said, giving a twirl.

"I do," Ben grinned.

Amy found her eyes drawn to Ty to see his reaction. "You look stunning," he said to her.

Amy felt the blood rush to her cheeks. She hurried to the door of the pick-up, glad that in the darkness no one could see her blush. "It's freezing out here," she said quickly, trying to disguise her embarrassment.

Ben held out his hand to Soraya and said, with a fake English accent, "May I escort you to your carriage, ma'am?"

Soraya giggled. "You may," she said, pretending to curtsy. Taking his hand, she let him help her into the pick-up. Amy and Ty followed her in.

It was a squeeze with all three of them in the front passenger seat and, sitting between Ty and Soraya, Amy was acutely aware of Ty's legs squashed against hers. Warmth radiated from him. She leant back and jumped slightly as their shoulders touched.

"Here," he said, moving in the seat to make more room for her.

"Thanks," Amy muttered, not daring to look him in the eye. The air was cold but her cheeks were burning. She looked down at her lap. Whatever was the matter with her?

The Grants lived in a sprawling mansion on the outskirts of town. A broad gravel driveway swept up to the grand front entrance decorated with an over-large holly wreath. On either side of the door were two tall Christmas trees, each covered with thousands of twinkling fairy lights. Candles flickered in every window. "Wow!" Soraya said. "It looks like a fairy palace."

"Or Santa's Christmas grotto at the shopping centre," Amy muttered. But even as she spoke, she had to admit that she was impressed. The place looked beautiful.

As they entered the house, the smell of balsam and pine

assaulted their nostrils. There were Christmas trees in every room and the mantelpieces were weighed down with swathes of dark green foliage and shiny red berries. Waiters bustled around with trays of drinks and beautifully prepared morsels of food – miniature quiches, smoked-salmon blinis, delicate asparagus spears, tiny hamburgers and Thai prawns. For the first time, Amy began to see why everyone went on so much about the Grants' Christmas party.

She looked around at the masses of people. "I wonder if Matt's here yet?"

"There!" said Soraya, nodding suddenly to a group standing by one of the Christmas trees. Matt was talking with Dan and Ashley, Jade and Brittany.

"Matt!" Amy called out.

Matt looked round. His handsome face broke into a smile. "Hey, Amy," he said, coming over. "You look great."

"Well, hi there!"

Amy turned round. Matt wasn't the only one who had seen them – Ashley had left her little group and was heading their way through the crowds. She was wearing a stunning silvery-green long dress that shimmered in the lights. With her pale-blonde hair cascading over her shoulders in a riot of artfully-styled curls, and her green eyes emphasized by layers of mascara, she looked like a mermaid.

"Hi, Ashley," Amy said. Reminding herself that this was the Grants' party, she forced herself to be polite. "You look ... lovely."

"Thank you." Ashley's eyes swept over Amy's outfit. "That's a nice dress — last year's, of course, but then styles like that don't really date, do they?" She smiled sweetly and turned to Ben and Ty. "Let me get you a drink."

Amy caught Soraya's eye and almost giggled. She knew Ashley's back-handed compliment had been intended to upset her but it didn't work with Amy; she didn't care whether her dress was fashionable or not.

Ashley waved a drinks waiter over and then looked up at Ben through her long lashes. "I'm so pleased *you* could come," she said.

"Thanks," Ben replied, smiling easily.

"You *must* come and meet my friends," Ashley said, putting a hand through his arm. "They're totally *dying* to meet you."

Shooting a rather helpless look at Amy, Ty and Soraya, Ben allowed himself to be led away.

Ty grinned at Amy. "Looks like that's Ben's evening taken care of."

Amy glanced at Soraya. The sparkle in her eyes had immediately disappeared. "We'll rescue him in a bit," Amy said quickly. "We won't let her monopolize him all night."

Just then, the live band started up in the far room. "Come on," Amy said, desperate to get Soraya to cheer up. "Let's go and dance!"

At first, Amy danced with Ty, Soraya and Matt as a foursome, but gradually Matt started to draw her away from the other two. "You really do look something this evening," he said.

Amy grinned at him. "Thanks."

For a few minutes, they danced without saying anything else, but Amy became conscious of Matt's eyes never leaving her face. As the song ended, the music changed tempo and slowed down.

Amy glanced round. "Well, I guess we should join the others," she said quickly. But before she could move, Matt had grabbed her hands.

"Dance with me properly," he whispered in her ear.

Amy swallowed. This wasn't what she wanted at all. "But it's a slow song," she said.

"I'd kind of noticed," Matt said, smiling at her. Still holding her hands, he tried to draw her closer. "Come on, Amy. You know how I feel about you."

Amy pulled back. Her heart was pounding now but she didn't want to make a scene. "Matt, I like you too," she stammered, desperately wishing she were somewhere — *anywhere* — else. "But if we started dating, it would change everything."

"Yeah — for the better," Matt said. He gripped her hand. "We'd be good together, Amy."

Amy saw the hope in his face. She didn't want to hurt him but she knew it would be really unfair to let him go on thinking there could be something between them when she just didn't like him like that. "Look, Matt, I really like you as a friend..."

Matt's face stiffened and, before she had a chance to go on to explain, he dropped her hand.

Amy saw the hurt in his eyes. "Matt..." she began.

Ignoring her, he swung round and started to walk away.

At just that moment, Soraya came bounding across the dance floor. "Ty and I are going to get something to eat," she said brightly, stopping in front of Matt. "Are you two coming?"

For a fraction of a second Amy thought Matt was going to brush past her, but then he shrugged. "Sure."

Breathing out a trembling sigh of relief, Amy watched him walk over to join Ty at the edge of the dance floor.

"You OK?" Soraya asked her in a low voice. "That looked as if it was getting awkward."

"It was," Amy said with feeling. "Thanks."

They followed Ty and Matt to the side of the dance floor where a long table had been set up with drinks and finger food on it. When they reached it, Ty looked at Amy. She was sure that he too had noticed what was going on, but he didn't say anything. Matt's face was hidden as he leant over the food table and filled a plate.

"Where's Ben?" Amy said.

"Where do you think?" Soraya sighed, nodding towards Ashley's group of friends.

Amy looked over. Ben was standing near the group with Ashley. She was trying to persuade him to dance. "Come on, you haven't danced all night," Amy heard her say.

Ben looked awkward. "Maybe later."

"Doesn't that girl know how to take no for an answer?" Amy said to Soraya.

Ashley flicked back her hair. "But I totally love this song. Come and dance with me." She took Ben's hand.

Ben gently freed himself. "No, thank you."

"What's the matter?" Ashley pouted. "Don't you like me?"

An embarrassed look crossed Ben's face. "Ashley, you've picked the wrong guy," he said. "I'm just not looking to get into a relationship at the moment."

Ashley stared at him and then drew back as if she'd been slapped. "A relationship!" she exclaimed, her face flushing hotly. "What! I only wanted a dance, you jerk!"

Ben stood there helplessly as Ashley stormed off.

"Well, that told her," Amy said with a giggle.

"Oh, yeah — what a great joke, Amy!" Amy swung round. Matt was standing a few paces behind her, glaring at her. "You know, Ashley might actually be upset. Did you stop to think about that?" He didn't give her time to let her answer. "No, of course not — it's all just a game to you, isn't it?"

Amy felt awful. She hadn't realized that Matt had been close enough to hear. "Matt..." she began, aware how insensitive her comment had been considering what had passed between them on the dance floor.

"Forget it, Amy," Matt said coldly as he walked off. "Just forget it."

Chapter Five

Amy looked at Soraya and Ty's stunned faces. "I'll go after him," she said quickly.

She set off across the dance floor. She felt awful and had to apologize to Matt. But then she stopped. Matt was walking up to Ashley. At first when Ashley turned to him her face was hard, but then he held out his hand. To Amy's astonishment, a look of gratitude crossed Ashley's face and, with a faint smile, she took Matt's hand and allowed him to lead her on to the dance floor.

Soraya came up behind her. "What's going on?" she asked, looking bewildered. Her eyes widened as she saw Matt and Ashley together on the dance floor. "What's Matt doing?" she gasped.

"Dancing," Amy snapped, a sharp pang of betrayal shooting through her as Matt's arms encircled Ashley's slender waist. He was supposed to be *her* friend.

"But he's dancing with *Ashley!*" Soraya said, as they watched Ashley's arms curve around Matt's neck. She swung round. "What's happened?" she demanded. "What made him lose it with you like that?"

"I don't know," Amy lied. She saw the disbelief in Soraya's eyes. "OK, I guess he might have been a bit upset because I wouldn't dance a slow dance with him," she admitted reluctantly.

"So he asked Ashley?" Soraya said, as if she still couldn't believe it. "But he doesn't even *like* Ashley."

"Well, he certainly doesn't seem to be giving that impression at the moment," Amy said sarcastically as she watched Matt draw Ashley closer.

However, as she spoke, the song came to an end and the music became faster again. Amy watched Matt and Ashley, expecting to see them go their separate ways. But they didn't. Matt said something to Ashley. She smiled and then they moved apart only slightly. Still holding hands, they started to dance again.

Amy had been watching Matt and Ashley for a few moments longer when she realized that Ty was standing beside her. Soraya was nowhere to be seen.

"Do you want to dance?" he asked.

Amy looked at him in surprise. "With you?"

Ty grinned. "No – with the tree in the corner."

Amy saw the teasing glint in his eyes and smiled. "OK," she said.

They found a space on the dance floor. Trying to forget about Matt dancing with Ashley, Amy let the music swell through her mind. As her body swayed in time with the beat, she glanced at Ty. His gaze was fixed on her face. As she met his warm eyes, Amy's heart somersaulted and she suddenly seemed to lose the ability to breathe. For a moment they just stared at each other and then, without saying a word, Ty stepped closer and took her hand.

The rest of the world seemed to swirl and fade away. Amy could think about nothing except the heat of Ty's fingers clasped around hers. They moved together in time with the music, their eyes fixed on each other's faces.

Amy was so engrossed that she didn't know how long they'd been dancing when Ben came up to them. "We've got some drinks and a table to sit at!" he shouted over the music. "Soraya's guarding it!"

Ty dropped Amy's hand.

"What?" Amy stammered to Ben, feeling like she'd just had a bucket of icy water thrown over her. She became suddenly aware of the crowd people around them, the sound of talking and laughing, of Ty standing opposite her and looking at her with an unreadable expression in his eyes.

Ben bellowed out his message again.

Amy glanced at Ty and saw his face smooth into its usual friendly expression. "Great," he said easily. "You coming, Amy?"

Amy forced herself to nod. "Sure." Her voice came out

high and breathless but neither Ben nor Ty seemed to notice. Taking a deep breath to calm her pounding heart, Amy followed them over to the table.

It was two o'clock in the morning when they finally got back to Heartland. Ty jumped out of the pick-up to let Amy out.

"Thanks for the lift, Ben," Amy said.

"No problem," Ben replied. "See you later."

Amy looked at Soraya. She was snuggled as close as she could get to Ben. "Ring me," Amy said, giving her a meaningful look. As far as she knew, nothing had happened between Ben and Soraya, but they had been talking and laughing together all evening and Amy wanted to know what Ben had been saying. She also wanted the chance to have a gossip about Matt and Ashley, who hadn't left each other's sides all night.

A grin twitched at Soraya's lips. "I will," she promised.

Amy got out. The frosty air stung her bare legs and her breath froze like smoke as it left her lips. "Night," she said to Ty, who was standing by the pick-up door. Since the moment on the dance floor they hadn't been alone together, but now she found herself looking into his eyes and felt a blush creep up her neck.

"Goodnight, Amy," Ty said softly.

Amy hesitated. She felt as if they were both waiting for something, but she didn't know what.

"See you later," she said breathlessly, and hurried indoors.

* * *

As she got into bed and turned off the light, Amy's thoughts raced back to the moment when she'd been dancing with Ty. Shutting her eyes, she could see his face as clearly as if he were there, could feel his fingers touching hers, could feel her heart pounding. She'd never felt like that before.

But this is Ty you're thinking about, she quickly reminded herself.

She curled her knees up to her chest. It was just so confusing. How *could* she feel like that about Ty, of all people? For a moment, she tried to envisage the two of them going out together – starting to date. But her mind seemed to hit a brick wall. She just couldn't imagine it. How could it possibly work?

It couldn't, she thought. *I see him every day. He's one of my best friends*. But still the memory of him holding her hand came back to her. She tried to push it away – after all, she didn't even know how Ty felt. It wasn't like he'd tried to kiss her or anything.

And if he had? she thought.

She stopped herself right there. She was being silly. Nothing was going to happen between her and Ty – *nothing*!

Four and a half hours later, Amy was woken by her alarm clock. She groaned and staggered out of bed. She was in the middle of mixing the feeds when Ty arrived.

"You look as good as I feel," he said, coming into the feed-room.

Amy jumped at the sound of his voice. "Hello," she said, hastily trying to cover her confusion. After the events of the night before, she sort of felt that he should look different – but he looked exactly the same as he did every other morning. "I can't believe I've only had four hours' sleep," she said.

"Me neither," Ty said, "But," his voice softened suddenly as his eyes met hers, "it was worth it."

Feeling suddenly flustered, Amy grabbed a pile of the feeds. "I'll go and get started on the back barn," she said.

For the rest of that morning, she avoided being alone with Ty. Trying not to think about the night before, she threw herself into the regular routine of cleaning the stalls and taking the horses out to the paddocks. Just before lunch, she was on her way up to fetch Moochie and Jake in when she saw Grandpa working on one of the gates. As he lifted a hammer to bang in a nail, he began to cough. He put the hammer down and leant against the fence, his shoulders shaking. He looked worse than ever.

Amy raced over. "Grandpa, you promised you'd stay inside today. You look awful."

With some effort, Jack straightened his shoulders. "I'm OK," he said. "I'll go inside once I've fixed the bar on this gate."

"I don't care about the gate, Grandpa, I want you to come inside now. You're not well." Amy stood with her hands on her hips, a determined glint in her eye.

"But if I don't do it now, it might not get done," Grandpa said, looking exasperated.

"It can wait." Amy said. "You're not doing it and I'm going to stand here until you agree!" She picked up the hammer so Jack couldn't use it.

"It looks like I've got no choice!" Grandpa said. He shrugged his shoulders. "All right, I'll go inside."

They walked back down to the yard together, Amy feeling very relieved that she had got Grandpa to agree to rest at last.

She heard the telephone ringing and then it stopped. A few seconds later, Lou opened the back door. "Amy! It's Soraya on the phone!"

Amy hurried to the kitchen and kicked her boots off, then took the phone from Lou. "Hello," she said, carrying the phone upstairs to her bedroom and shutting the door. "How are you?"

"Fine," Soraya said and Amy could hear the grin in her voice. "Oh, Amy, I've got so much to tell you."

"You and Ben?" Amy said eagerly.

"Yes!" Soraya said. "Do you remember when you and Ty were dancing?"

Did she remember? Amy didn't think she'd ever forget. "Yes," she said, trying not to think about that time on the dance floor.

"Well, did you notice that when Ben and I disappeared to get some drinks we were gone quite a long time?" Soraya said.

Not wanting to admit that she hadn't noticed at all, Amy quickly lied. "Yes, yes, of course I did."

"Well…" Soraya stopped.

"Go on," Amy urged.

"Well, there was a huge queue for drinks so we went outside on to the veranda for a bit." Soraya sighed dreamily. "It was, like, totally romantic. There were loads of stars in the sky and just me and Ben standing there."

"And?" Amy said in an agony of impatience. "What happened?"

"Well, nothing happened exactly," Soraya admitted. "We just stayed there and talked. He told me all about how he felt growing up on his aunt's farm rather than with his parents and about how he feels he's now getting to know his mom all over again. It was so special. He said he felt he could really talk to me."

"Yes, but did he kiss you?" Amy asked, keen to get to the important point.

"No," Soraya admitted. "He said that he's got so much stuff going on in his life with his mom that he just doesn't want to date anyone just yet. But I don't care. I'll wait. I'll just be his friend at the moment if that's what he wants." Amy could hear the happiness in Soraya's voice. "He's so totally wonderful. When he dropped me off at home he said he'd really enjoyed the evening and that maybe we could go out one night."

"On a date!" Amy exclaimed.

"Well, not a date exactly," Soraya said. "But you ever know — it could lead to that."

"That's brilliant!" Amy said. "Just think how mad Ashley will be if you start dating him!"

"Talking about Ashley, what do you think about her and Matt?" Soraya said eagerly.

"It has to be a one-night thing," Amy said. "He can't possibly *like* her."

Soraya suddenly sounded more serious. "But what if they do start dating? Do you think that'll mean she'll hang round with us?"

"They won't start dating," Amy said. "Matt's got more taste."

Soraya didn't say anything.

"He has!" Amy insisted, trying to suppress a vision of Matt and Ashley going round together at school.

"Well, I guess we'll see tomorrow," Soraya said.

After Soraya rang off, Amy sat in her room thinking about what Soraya had said. Surely Matt and Ashley wouldn't start dating — would they?

She looked at the phone and then punched in Matt's number.

"Hello, Mrs Trewin," Amy said when Matt's mom answered. "It's Amy. Is Matt there?"

"I think you're in luck," Mrs Trewin said. "I just heard him get up. Let me call him for you." Amy heard Mrs Trewin shouting for Matt and then she came back on the phone. "It must have been some party last night," she said with a laugh. "He's not been out of his room all morning."

"It was," Amy said.

Just then, Matt took the phone from his mom.

"Hi," Amy said brightly.

"Hello." Matt's voice sounded guarded.

Amy felt suddenly awkward. "It was good last night, wasn't it?" she said.

"I enjoyed it," Matt replied briefly.

There was a pause. Amy longed to ask about Ashley but Matt sounded so cool and reserved that she didn't quite dare. For the first time since they had become friends, she found herself searching for something to say to him. "So ... what are you doing today?" she said at last.

"Just stuff," Matt said non-committally.

He didn't expand and there was another uncomfortable pause. "Right, well, I better get going," Amy said. "I ... I just thought I'd ring to say hi."

"Yeah," Matt said. "See you tomorrow at school, then."

As Amy put the phone down, she realized that her face was red. Matt had sounded like he hadn't wanted to talk to her at all. She remembered how hurt he had looked when she had been laughing with Soraya after Ben had turned Ashley down. More than anything, she wished that she could take that moment back. Matt was her friend and, although she didn't want to go out with him, she had never meant to upset him.

He'll be OK tomorrow, she told herself, trying to be positive. *He'll have forgotten about it by then.*

But on the bus the next day, she couldn't help feeling nervous as they reached Matt's stop. Would he still be mad about the party? Matt's tall figure got on and, to Amy's relief, he made his way to the seat in front of her and Soraya, just like he usually did.

"Hi," he said. He sounded normal but Amy noticed how his eyes slipped quickly away from hers as he greeted them.

"Hello," Soraya grinned, not seeming to notice the slight restraint in Matt's voice. Amy had felt too embarrassed to tell her about the phone conversation she'd had with Matt. "So, what were you up to on Saturday night with Ashley?" Soraya teased.

Matt looked uncomfortable. "We were just dancing."

"So are you going to start dating her?" Soraya said. "Go on – tell us."

Amy saw how awkward Matt was looking. "Of course Matt's not going to start dating Ashley," she said quickly, wanting to stop Soraya's teasing.

It was the wrong thing to say. Matt turned on her. "What do you mean, I'm not?" he demanded.

"Well, I mean, it's *Ashley*," Amy said, taken aback by the anger in his eyes.

Matt glared at her, obviously misinterpreting her words.

"It may be hard for you to conceive, Amy, but some people do actually find me attractive."

Amy stared at him. "I didn't mean that, I just..."

Matt got to his feet. "You know, sometimes you can be so full of yourself, Amy," he said, and stalked off to sit further down the bus.

Amy and Soraya looked at each other in stunned silence for a moment and then Amy jumped to her feet. "Matt," she said, following him. "I didn't mean that she wouldn't find you attractive."

Suddenly Matt looked very weary. "Look, just forget it," he said. "I don't want to talk about it." Opening his bag, he took out a book and began to read.

Amy was suddenly aware of the curious looks they were getting from the other students around them. She hesitated, hoping Matt would look up, but his head stayed resolutely bent over his book. With her cheeks burning, she made her way back down the bus.

At school that day, Matt hardly said a word to Amy. He hung around with Ashley and her friends. Every so often; Ashley would link her arm through his and look triumphantly over in Amy's direction.

"I don't know what she's looking at me like that for," Amy muttered to Soraya at lunchtime. "Anyone would think that I wanted to go out with Matt myself."

"Sure you're not jealous?" Soraya said slyly.

"Jealous!" Amy exclaimed. "Of course I'm not jealous. Matt can do what he likes!"

But despite her words she had to admit that she missed Matt. Not romantically, like Soraya meant, but they'd been friends since sixth grade and it felt strange to see him hanging around with other people – particularly Ashley and her friends.

By the time Amy got home that afternoon, she was in a very bad mood. She dumped her bag in the empty kitchen and went upstairs to get changed. Lou was in her bedroom, sorting out clothes for her trip. "Had a good day?" she asked, as Amy went past.

"No," Amy replied abruptly.

"Oh," Lou said. She came to her door. "Do you want to talk about it?" she said.

"No," Amy said again and went into her bedroom, pointedly shutting the door behind her.

She went to the window. The cold grey sky seemed to press down on the muddy fields. Sundance and Jasmine were grazing in the field by the back barn. Amy suddenly frowned. Grandpa was working on the gate again. As he bent to pick up some nails, she saw him start to cough. He leant weakly against the fence, his shoulders shaking.

"Oh, Grandpa," Amy muttered, exasperated.

She pulled off the jumper she'd been wearing for school and grabbed a sweatshirt, determined to go straight out and tell him to come inside. But then she saw Grandpa stagger. He grasped at the fence, fighting for breath, and suddenly his knees appeared to sag beneath him. Clutching his chest, he sank to the ground.

"Lou!" Amy screamed, throwing her top down and running to the door. "Lou! Come quick!"

Chapter Six

"Dial 911!" Lou shouted over her shoulder as she ran down the stairs and out of the house. "Call an ambulance!"

Her heart pounding, Amy grabbed the portable phone in the kitchen. It only took a few seconds to get through to the emergency services. "Ambulance please!" Amy gasped when an operator answered. All the time, her eyes never stopped looking at Grandpa's bent-over body.

By now, Lou had reached him. Amy saw Lou's arms go round his shoulders, saw her turn and yell for Ty and Ben.

"Name please," a voice spoke in Amy's ear.

"Fleming — Amy Fleming," she burst out.

"Address?"

Amy gabbled out the address.

"And what seems to be the problem, Amy?" the woman on the other end of the phone calmly asked.

"It's my grandpa," Amy said, barely able to get the words out. "He's collapsed."

She was asked more questions – what exactly had happened, whether Grandpa was conscious, how old she was, who was with her. She answered them almost without thinking as she watched Lou, Ty and Ben help Grandpa to his feet. Half-carrying him, they brought him back to the house.

"An ambulance is on its way," the woman said. "I want to know as much as you can tell me about your grandpa's condition so I can help you to help him while you wait for the ambulance to arrive. Now, does he have a fever?"

"I don't know," Amy replied anxiously. "Hang on…"

Lou came through the door, opening it wide so Ty and Ben could help Grandpa inside. "Lou! They want to know about Grandpa's condition. Has he got a fever?" Amy gasped.

"Here, I'll talk to them." Lou grabbed the phone from her. "Lou Fleming here," she said.

Amy looked at Grandpa. He was conscious but his lips were blue and he was breathing in quick shallow gasps. Beads of sweat stood out on his forehead.

"Get a chair, Amy!" Ty said.

As Amy dragged a chair out and helped Ty and Ben lower Grandpa into it, she heard Lou answering the woman's questions. Despite her obvious concern, Lou sounded brisk and in control. "I see," she said, scribbling notes on the pad. "Keep him warm, change his clothes if they're damp, give him fluids if he'll take them. And how long did you say the ambulance would be?"

Amy crouched beside Grandpa's side. "It's going to be OK. The ambulance will be here soon."

"No ambulance. I'll be all right." Grandpa said, wheezing between each sentence. His usually sharp blue eyes looked dazed and confused. "Got to fix the gate."

"The gate!" Amy exclaimed. "The gate doesn't matter, Grandpa!"

A spasm of coughs burst from Jack and he bent over, his face screwed up in pain.

Amy couldn't bear it. "What's the matter with him?" she cried, rounding on Ty and Ben.

"Pneumonia." There was a click from behind them as Lou replaced the receiver. They all turned to look at her. "That's what the woman thinks from our descriptions." She hurried to Grandpa's side. "Come on, we've got to keep him warm and dry until the ambulance arrives."

The next few hours passed in a blur for Amy. The ambulance seemed to take forever to arrive. However, when it did, the paramedics immediately assessed the situation. Grandpa was lifted into the ambulance and given oxygen via a mask. Then the doors shut and the ambulance set off for the hospital. Leaving Ben and Ty to see to the horses, Amy and Lou followed in Lou's car. Neither of them spoke much on the way. Staring out of the window, Amy just kept seeing

Grandpa collapsing on the ground, his face contorting with pain.

At the hospital, Grandpa was taken away immediately and they simply had to wait. A last, a young, female doctor came to find them and confirmed that Mr Bartlett did indeed have pneumonia.

"So what exactly does that mean?" Lou demanded.

"Well, as you may know, pneumonia is a serious inflammation of the lungs," Dr Jane Marshall explained. "The air sacs in the lungs fill with liquid and this stops the correct amount of oxygen reaching the blood," she paused, watching them to see if they were following. "Your grandfather has a bacterial form of pneumonia. It can affect people of all ages but it's most likely to affect people whose immune system has been weakened in some way by an illness. When a person's resistance is lowered, the bacteria that normally live in the throat can work their way into the lungs where they cause the air sacs to inflame."

Amy thought about the cold that Grandpa had picked up when helping Melody to foal. "Grandpa has had a bad cold for several weeks," she interrupted. "He didn't rest and it just got worse. Could that have weakened his immune system?"

"It might have done," Dr Marshall replied, nodding.

"So, how long will it take for him to get better?" Lou said quickly.

"It all depends upon how he responds to treatment," Dr Marshall said. "The inflammation is very severe, which is why he's got such a high temperature and is in such pain. We're giving him antibiotics to combat the infection and painkillers to help ease the pain in his chest from coughing. He's also having help to get his oxygen levels back to normal. Providing he responds to the treatment and there are no complications, we're probably looking at a hospital stay of about a week."

"Can we see him?" Lou asked.

"Yes, but just briefly," Dr Marshall said. "We're still trying to stabilize his condition."

Amy and Lou followed her down a succession of long white corridors. At last, the doctor stopped outside a door. "He's in here," she said.

Amy took a quick look through the glass in the door. Grandpa was lying in bed on his back; his eyes were closed. Long, thin tubes travelled from machines into his arm and nose.

Dr Marshall opened the door. "You can go in," she said quietly.

They walked into the room. Lou sat down by the bed and took Grandpa's still hand. "Hello, Grandpa," she murmured.

Amy followed her. Standing beside Lou's chair, she saw Grandpa's eyelids blink. "Lou?" he whispered hoarsely, turning to look at her.

Lou squeezed his hand. "Yes, Grandpa, I'm here. So's Amy."

Grandpa's clouded blue eyes found Amy. She felt a lump

of tears form in her throat as she saw the confusion in his face. "Hello, Grandpa," she said, longing to hug him but not quite daring to because of the tubes.

"Where am I?" Grandpa asked.

"In the hospital," Lou replied. "You've got pneumonia and you need to stay here a while, until you get better."

Amy half-expected Grandpa to object but his illness seemed to have drained all the fight from him. He nodded wordlessly.

Lou squeezed his hand. "We're going home now. You need to rest." She leant forward and kissed his cheek. "But we'll come back tomorrow. You take care now."

She stood up and let Amy take her place. "Bye, Grandpa," Amy whispered. "We love you."

A faint smile caught at the corners of Grandpa's mouth. "I love you both, too."

Amy and Lou got back to Heartland at ten o'clock that evening. They found the lights on and Ben and Ty waiting for them.

"How's Jack?" Ty asked as soon as they got out of the car.

"They're still trying to stabilize him but they think he's going to be OK," Lou said. She explained about the pneumonia, her voice as brisk as the doctor's. "We can go back first thing in the morning."

"Well, don't worry about the horses," Ben said. "We'll see to them, won't we, Ty?"

Ty nodded.

"Thanks," Lou said, gratefully. "That would be a real help."

"Do you want us to do anything now?" Ty asked, looking from her to Amy.

"No, we'll be fine," Lou said. "You two go home."

Ben said goodnight and went over to his pick-up but Ty paused by Amy. "How are you doing?"

She shrugged. She had a feeling that if she spoke she would start to cry.

Ty squeezed her shoulder. "Look, I'll see you tomorrow," he said, and walked to his truck.

As she watched his tail-lights disappear down the drive, Amy felt tears spill down her cheeks.

"Hey, Amy," Lou said, noticing and hugging her. "Don't cry. You heard what the doctor said. Grandpa's going to be OK."

Amy wiped her sleeve across her eyes. "But it was just seeing him like that, Lou — with all those tubes."

"I know," Lou said. "But he'll be out in a week or two." She took Amy's hands. "Come on, Amy, we need to be strong — for Grandpa."

Amy stayed off school the next day. She and Lou went to the hospital in the morning and found Grandpa looking a bit brighter. He was still pale but his skin had lost the horrible blue-white pallor of the day before. A drip led into his arm but he no longer had a tube connected to his nose.

Lou sat down next to him and Amy sat on the edge of the bed. "How are you feeling?" Lou asked him.

"Better," Grandpa said weakly

"Good," Lou told him. "Now, you're going to do exactly what the doctor says, aren't you? You're going to rest and get better."

Jack nodded. "I've learnt my lesson." He looked at Amy. "How's everything on the yard?"

"Fine," she reassured him. "Ty and Ben are seeing to everything."

"You're not to worry about a thing," Lou said quickly. "I'm going to cancel my trip to England. We'll easily manage till you come back."

Jack stared at her. "No, Lou – don't cancel it, not for me."

"Don't be silly, Grandpa," Lou said. "I'm not going away while you're in hospital."

"But I don't want you to stay because of me." Grandpa pulled himself up against his pillows as Lou opened her mouth to argue. "No, I mean it, Lou," he insisted. "I want you to go." The exertion of sitting up made him start to cough. He bent over, his face turning white as he grasped at his chest.

Amy looked at Lou in alarm. Lou quickly picked up a glass of water from beside the bed. "Here, Grandpa, drink this."

Grandpa swallowed a few sips. "Please," he said weakly, as he caught his breath and his coughs died away. "Go to England like you'd decided."

Lou shook her head. "I couldn't."

"Go," Grandpa said, starting to look agitated again. "I won't feel happy till I know you're going, Lou."

Lou hesitated. She looked at Amy, who shrugged. "OK, Grandpa – I'll go," Lou said slowly.

Amy stared at her sister.

"Good," Grandpa whispered, a look of relief crossing his face as he sank back against the pillows. His chest moved up and down in short, shallow breaths.

"We've tired you," Lou said, looking worried. "We'd better leave."

But Jack shook his head. "No. I want to tell you something first."

"It can wait," Amy said, standing up. "We'll come back later, Grandpa."

"I want to tell you now," Grandpa insisted. "It's about your parents."

Amy sat down again slowly, wondering what he was going to tell them.

Jack took a wheezing breath. "It's something your mother never told you. I realized this morning that, if anything ever happened to me, you might never know."

"Know what, Grandpa?" Lou asked.

Grandpa paused for a moment. "There's no easy way to say this," he said, looking from one sister to the other, "but three years ago your parents got a divorce."

Amy stared at him. "A divorce! They can't have done." She

saw the shock on Lou's face. "Mom would have told us!"

"She didn't tell anyone apart from me," Jack said. "Your father initiated the divorce. Your mom didn't want to agree – despite everything, she still loved him – but, as you know, she'd already turned down his attempts at a reconciliation and I think she probably felt she had no choice."

Amy struggled to get her head round the idea. She'd always thought her mom and dad had stayed married. *Well, what does it matter?* she thought. *It's not like they were ever going to get back together.* But it did matter and she knew it. Being divorced seemed so much more final than just being separated. "Why didn't you tell us before, Grandpa?" she asked, trying to understand.

Jack sighed. "I wanted to respect your mother's wishes," he said. "She didn't tell you when she was alive so I didn't see how I could after she died. I feel like I've betrayed her. But I couldn't keep it from you – you have the right to know."

There was silence for a moment and then Lou spoke. "Thank you for telling us," she said, squeezing Grandpa's hand. "You did the right thing."

Jack looked at her anxiously. "It's not going to stop you going to England?"

Lou shook her head. "Divorced or not, he's still my daddy." She smiled. "The only thing that will stop me going is if you don't start getting better."

Looking as if a weight had been taken off his shoulders, Jack leant back against the pillows. "Oh, I'll get better," he said, smiling weakly back at her. "I'll be out of here in no time — just you wait and see."

Chapter Seven

"So what's the news?" Ty said when he and Ben met Amy and Lou after they'd pulled into Heartland's driveway.

"It looks like Grandpa will be in hospital for at least a week," Lou explained, as she stepped out of her car. "But then, providing there are no complications, he can come home and recuperate here."

"That's great news," Ben said, looking relieved.

Lou smiled. "Yes, it is."

Not a single muscle in Lou's face betrayed the impact of Grandpa's recent announcement. Amy wasn't able to hide her feelings so well. "I'm going to get changed," she said, just wanting to be on her own.

In her bedroom, she sank down on her unmade bed. Mom and Dad were divorced. She thought about the letter her father had written to her mother, begging for a reconciliation.

I'll never stop loving you, he had written in that letter. She picked up the photograph of her mom and Pegasus that she kept beside her bed.

As always when she saw that photograph, she'd have given anything to have her mom back for half an hour – to talk to her again, to tell her how much she loved her. But this time she would ask her mom questions. Why did she keep Daddy's letter secret? And why hadn't she told them about the divorce?

When Amy finally went back downstairs she found Lou, Ty and Ben in the kitchen having coffee.

"Do you want some?" Lou asked, gesturing towards the coffee pot.

Amy shook her head. She didn't feel like talking. "I'll go and get started on the grooming."

Ty jumped to his feet. "I'll join you," he said, dumping his coffee mug in the sink and following her outside.

"Are you all right?" he asked as they walked up the yard.

Amy nodded. She didn't want to talk, even to Ty.

Ty looked up at the sky where dark rainclouds were gathering on the horizon. "We should leave the grooming," he suggested, "and take Daybreak to the field before that rain sets in."

"OK," Amy agreed, feeling relieved – she knew that if she was with Daybreak she wouldn't have a chance to think about anything else. And right now, that was just what she wanted.

They fetched Melody's and Daybreak's halters from the tack-room and went up to the back barn. As she always did before attempting to lead Daybreak out, Amy spent five minutes running her hands over the filly's body and legs.

Daybreak seemed quieter than usual. "She's being good," Amy said to Ty, who was holding the filly's head. "Maybe the vetiver oil's working."

"Or maybe she's not very well," Ty said, pointing to Daybreak's muzzle. "Look."

Amy joined him and saw, for the first time, that Daybreak had a runny nose. She felt worried. She knew that any illness in a young foal had to be watched carefully: foals under eight weeks old don't share the ability older horses have to fight off disease. "I'll check her temperature," she said.

Amy fetched the thermometer. "Thirty-eight degrees," she said, checking the reading twice to make sure. "So it's normal."

"Well, I guess we don't need to call Scott out just yet then," Ty said. "But we'd better keep an eye on her for the next few days."

Later that morning, Amy saw Scott's jeep coming up the driveway. "Amy!" he said, as he got out of the car looking worried. "Ty rang me this morning and told me about Jack. I came as soon as I could. How is he?"

"He's a bit better," Amy said. "The hospital said that he'd probably be out in a week." She was just going to ask him to take a look at Daybreak when the back door opened and Lou came out.

"Scott, what are you doing here?" she said in surprise.

"Ty told me the news," Scott said, and walked over to her. "I came as soon as I could." He held out his arms. Lou stepped forward and Scott's arms folded around her. Bending his head, he kissed her hair.

It was such an intimate moment that Amy felt awkward witnessing it. She started to back away.

Scott noticed and broke away from Lou. "It must have been terrible for both of you," he said, including Amy in his glance. "So what exactly did the hospital say?"

Lou explained. "I don't know how we're going to make him take it easy when he comes out." She looked at Amy. "You mustn't let him do anything on the yard while I'm away."

"I won't," Amy said. She saw Scott frown.

"What do you mean, when you're away?" he asked Lou.

Lou's cheeks flushed pink. "I'm ... I'm still flying to London tomorrow."

Scott stared at her in astonishment. "What? When Jack's in hospital?"

"Grandpa wants me to go," Lou said quickly. "He knows how important this is to me. My life just feels empty without Daddy."

Amy saw Scott's jaw tighten. "I see," he said flatly. "I didn't realize you felt that way."

"I want to stay — really, I do," Lou went on, "but Grandpa won't hear of it — he's made me promise I'll go."

"*Made* you?" Scott snapped angrily. "Jack would never make you do anything, Lou. You know that. This is your choice. Don't try and pretend it's not."

Lou looked astonished at his outburst. "Scott…"

"No, Lou," Scott interrupted icily. "If you feel you should go chasing halfway round the world after your father when the man who has *really* cared for you for the last twelve years is sick in hospital, then that's fine — it's your decision. Just don't try and justify it to me." Scott's face was thunderous as he strode down to his jeep, slammed the door shut and drove away.

Amy looked quickly at Lou. She was staring after Scott's car with a shocked expression on her face and then tears suddenly filled her eyes and she ran into the house.

Amy followed her. "Lou?" she said tentatively, going over to where her sister was standing by the kitchen table.

"I can't believe Scott just said those things!" Lou exclaimed. She sank down in a chair. "Of course I don't want to leave Grandpa while he's ill, but he understands — you heard him today — it will only make him unhappy if I stay."

Well, maybe it wouldn't if Grandpa thought that you really wanted to stay, Amy thought to herself, but looking at the pain on Lou's face made her bite back her words.

"If I could be in two places at once, I would be," Lou said, shaking her head. "But I have to go to England. You know that."

Amy didn't know what to say.

Lou stared at her. "You agree with Scott, don't you?" she said. "You think I should stay."

"I don't," Amy lied quickly, not wanting to upset Lou even more. "You *should* go to England, Lou. Grandpa will get better soon and it'll only make him feel guilty if you stay." Even to her own ears her words sounded false but Lou didn't seem to notice. She nodded, looking slightly comforted.

"You're right. I mean it's not like I'm going to be gone long." She managed a smile. "Thanks, Amy. It's good to know I've got your support."

Amy smiled, trying to ignore the voice in her head that said: *Just tell her that you think she should stay.*

Lou sighed. "I just wish Scott could be so understanding." A frown crossed her face. "I can't believe he blew up at me like that."

"He was probably just hurt," Amy said. She saw her sister's surprised expression. "You did tell him that your life felt empty, Lou. That can't have made him feel too great."

Lou looked at her in astonishment. "But I didn't mean that my life was bad, just that it sort of feels incomplete without Daddy."

"It didn't come out quite like that," Amy said.

"But Scott *knows* how important he is to me," Lou said. "He's not that dumb." She shook her head and stood up. "You'll see – he'll come round in the end."

* * *

Amy got up at six o'clock the next morning to see Lou leave. "Now, you've got Marnie's phone number," Lou checked as she put her bags in the car.

Amy nodded. "What time do you think she'll arrive?"

"About five o'clock," Lou said.

"What about you?" Amy said. "Where can I contact you?"

"I'll ring from London when I get in," Lou said. "I'll be staying one night in a hotel near the airport and then I'll travel to Gloucestershire – where Daddy lives." She gave Amy a slightly nervous look. "I'm not sure where I'll be staying after that."

Amy hugged her. "Good luck."

"Thanks," Lou said, hugging her back. "Now, remember to go back to school tomorrow."

"I will," Amy sighed. They'd agreed that she would stay off school until Marnie had arrived. "Though I don't see the point of going back. Term ends soon anyhow."

Lou smiled at her. "You can still go back until then."

They embraced for a long moment and then Lou got in the car and drove off. Amy waved until her sister's car disappeared from sight, then she looked around. It was still dark and everywhere suddenly seemed very quiet. She went into the house, trying to get used to the strange sensation of being on her own.

Back in the kitchen, the silence pressed down on her. She switched the radio on and sat down at the table, wondering what to do. She picked up the latest issue of the local paper and she tried to read, but the words just wouldn't sink in. So much had happened in the last few days – the Grants' party, Grandpa going into hospital and now Lou leaving. She shook her head. It felt like the Grants' party was weeks ago.

At last, she gave up trying to read, pulled on her jacket and boots and she went outside to get started on the horses.

When Ben arrived, he volunteered to finish off the jobs that Grandpa had been working on. Amy agreed, thinking that at least then Grandpa wouldn't be tempted to go outside when he came home from hospital, but it did mean that she and Ty had to do the horses on their own. The phone – usually answered by Lou – seemed to ring constantly with enquiries from prospective clients and people looking for horses to re-home. As Amy answered the ringing for the sixth time that morning, she silently thanked Lou for getting the portable phone. How had they managed before?

Walking into the feed-room after the last call, Amy was reminded that she needed to ring the feed merchants because the stocks were running low. That was when she began to realize, for the first time, just how much Heartland's day-to-day running depended on her sister.

At lunchtime, Ty drove Amy to the hospital.

"Did Lou get off all right?" Grandpa asked them as they sat down.

"Yes, she left at six this morning," Amy answered.

Grandpa nodded. "And how's everything going?"

"We're managing just fine," Amy told him. "Ben's been fixing the fences this morning and Ty and I have just about got all the horses done," she lied, trying not to think about the five stalls that still needed to be mucked out, the unswept yard and the fact that it looked like none of the horses were going to get worked that day.

Grandpa looked relieved. "Good," he said.

Amy looked at him in concern. He was paler than the day before, and as he coughed she saw his knuckles clench the bed sheets. "How are you feeling?" she asked.

It seemed to take an effort but Grandpa managed to smile. "I'm on the mend," he said. "Don't you worry about me. You've got enough to think about, with looking after the yard."

But Amy wasn't convinced and, as they left the hospital, she told Ty that she wanted to find a doctor. They asked at the reception desk and were told to wait. They had been waiting on the hard plastic chairs in the lobby for fifteen minutes when, to Amy's relief, Dr Marshall came to find them.

"I'm afraid your grandfather's not responding quite as well as we had hoped to the medication," she admitted to Amy. She saw Amy's face pale. "But, please – be assured we're monitoring his progress carefully."

Amy's throat felt dry. "Will ... will he still be able to come home soon?" she asked, trying to sound calm.

Dr Marshall looked at her sympathetically. "I'm afraid I

can't say at the moment; we'll just have to see how he gets on over the next few days."

Amy nodded, unable to speak.

"Do you have any other questions?" the doctor asked.

Ty looked at Amy, who shook her head. "Thank you," he said to the doctor.

Amy followed him out of the hospital, her stomach churning with worry.

"Jack'll be all right, Amy," Ty said, looking at her white face as they went outside.

Desperately wanting to believe him, Amy nodded.

"If it was anything more serious the doctor would have told you," Ty reassured her.

Amy took comfort from his words. "Yeah," she whispered, trying to be positive. But she couldn't help thinking that Grandpa was even more sick than she'd imagined.

Chapter Eight

Just as they were finishing feeding the horses that evening, a red sports car came up the drive. "Marnie!" Amy exclaimed as it stopped in front of the house and a tall, slim woman in her twenties got out. Dumping the hay nets she was carrying on the ground, Amy raced down the yard.

"Hi, Amy!" Marnie said, hugging her. Marnie's blonde hair bounced on her shoulders as she looked round. "Wow!" she said. "It's so good to be back."

Amy grinned, feeling really happy for the first time in days. She knew Marnie loved Heartland – that was one of the reasons why she liked her so much. "I love your car," she said, looking at the shiny new sports car.

"Well, there have to be some perks to working in the city," Marnie said. She took a deep breath of the frosty air. "Though I have to admit that I have my doubts now I'm here again."

"Do you want a hand with your bags?" Amy offered.

Marnie glanced at the hay nets lying on the ground. "No, you go ahead and finish what you were doing. I can manage – am I in the same room as last time?"

Amy nodded. It was her mom's old room. "Just make yourself at home," she said.

Marnie smiled at her. "That'll be easy. This place feels like home already."

After unpacking and going round the yard, saying hi to all the horses and to Ben and Ty, Marnie set about making supper. "I'll go shopping tomorrow," she said, peering into the almost empty fridge. "But for tonight, I could make us some pasta with a..." she looked in the store cupboards, "tuna, tomato and olive sauce. How does that sound?"

"Great," Amy said.

"Do Ty and Ben want to stay for supper?" Marnie asked. "I can easily make enough to feed all of us."

Amy went to ask. "They both said they'd love to," she said, returning to find that Marnie was already preparing for four hungry people. "They're just finishing off in the feed-room," she smiled.

Marnie tossed her a tin of olives. "Then let's get this food on the go. You start chopping those and I'll put the pasta on."

Amy sat down at the table and set to work. A few minutes later, Ben and Ty came in. They shrugged off their jackets, washed their hands and began to help. The kitchen, which only that morning had seemed so silent and empty, was now suddenly bustling with life.

In the middle of the supper preparations, the phone rang. It was Lou.

"Lou!" Amy exclaimed. "Hi! Where are you?" Hearing her exclamation, Marnie, Ty and Ben immediately quietened down.

"I'm in London," Lou replied. "At the hotel."

"How was the flight?" Amy asked.

"We were a bit late getting in, but it was OK," Lou said. "How's Grandpa?"

Amy hesitated. She didn't want to worry Lou now she was so far away. "Fine," she said.

"That's good." Lou sounded very relieved. "I haven't been able to stop thinking about him."

"Marnie's here," Amy said quickly, wanting to get off the subject of Grandpa. "Do you want to say hello?"

"Yeah!" Lou replied.

Amy held the phone out to Marnie, who handed Ben the cheese to grate while she spoke to her best friend. "How are you doing?" she said, taking the phone off Amy.

Lou and Marnie spoke for a few minutes and then Marnie handed the receiver back to Amy.

"I'd better go," Lou said. "This phone bill's going to cost me the earth. Give Grandpa a big hug for me."

"I will," Amy promised.

"And wish me luck for tomorrow," Lou said, sounding

nervous. "I've hired a car and I'm going to drive over to Gloucestershire to Daddy's house in the morning."

Amy's heart flipped. With everything that had been happening, she had pushed the thought that Lou might be meeting their father the next day to the back of her mind. "Good luck," she said.

"I'll ring you tomorrow night and tell you all about it," Lou said. "Bye for now."

"Yeah, bye," Amy said and with a click Lou was gone.

"Lou sounds good," Marnie said to her as she replaced the handset on the charger.

Amy nodded slowly. "Yeah." She chewed on a fingernail. "She's going to see Daddy tomorrow."

Marnie looked at her quizzically. Amy thought she was going to say something but she didn't. Instead she swung back into action. "OK, supper's almost ready," she said, taking the cheese grater from Ben. "Someone get the drinks organized, then we can all sit down and eat."

After supper, Marnie and Amy went to the hospital. Grandpa was lying in bed, looking pale and tired. Talking seemed to hurt him and he didn't say much, but he was evidently pleased to see Marnie.

"I didn't realize he was quite so ill," Marnie said, as they walked back to the car. "Lou seemed to think he was getting better when she rang me last night."

"He was," Amy said. "But now I'm not so sure. Ty and I

spoke to a doctor this morning and she said he's not responding to his medication."

"You didn't mention it to Lou when she rang this evening?" Marnie said.

"No," Amy admitted, wondering whether Marnie would think she'd done the right thing. "I didn't want to worry her."

"That was probably wise," Marnie said reassuringly. "After all, she can't do anything about it while she's in England." She frowned. "Still, if he does get much worse you should probably tell her."

Hoping that it wouldn't come to that, Amy nodded. "Yeah, I will."

Amy didn't sleep well that night. One minute she was thinking about Grandpa in hospital and the next she was thinking about Lou – in just a few hours' time Lou was going to see Daddy. What would happen?

By the morning her stomach was knotted with tension. "Maybe I won't go to school today," she said to Marnie as they got breakfast together. "If I don't go, I could visit Grandpa this morning."

"Why don't you give the hospital a ring and see how he is?" Marnie suggested. "He might be feeling better."

Amy agreed. But when she got through to the ward, she was told that she couldn't be put through. "I'm sorry, but he's asleep," the nurse said. "He's had a disturbed night and he needs to rest."

"Can I come and see him?" Amy asked quickly.

"It might be best if you wait till later," the nurse replied. "He really needs to be kept quiet. Maybe late this afternoon."

"What did they say?" Marnie asked, her eyes anxiously scanning Amy's face.

Amy told her. "I'm definitely *not* going to school," she said.

"But it'll keep your mind off worrying," Marnie said. She must have seen the uncertainty on Amy's face. "Look, if there's any news, I'll phone the school right away," she promised. "If I don't hear anything then I'll come and collect you after school and we can go straight to the hospital then."

Amy reluctantly gave in. In a sense she knew that Marnie was right. She would only think about Grandpa and Lou all day if she were at home.

Marnie gave Amy a ride to school. "I promise I'll ring if the hospital calls," she said as Amy got out of the car. "Try not to worry."

Amy walked slowly into school. She was so wrapped up in her own thoughts that she hardly noticed Ashley and Jade standing nearby.

"Hi, Amy," Ashley said, following her. "How's that foal?" She sniggered. "Still too much for you to control?" Since she had lost interest in Ben, she had dropped all pretence of being nice to Amy. "Maybe you should send her someplace where they really know about horses."

Amy stopped. For a moment she felt her temper rise but, as she looked into Ashley's taunting face, she suddenly switched off. "Yeah, whatever, Ashley," she said, showing no emotion as she walked away. But not before she had caught the look of triumph in Ashley's eyes. She ignored it. Right now, she didn't have the energy for a fight. Walking round the corner, she almost bumped into Matt.

"Amy!" he exclaimed. "Scott told me about your grandpa being in hospital. I'm really sorry."

"Thanks," Amy said briefly, walking on.

"Look," Matt said following her. "I'm sorry about Monday as well. I shouldn't have gone off at you like that."

"It doesn't matter," Amy said flatly. "Just forget it."

Matt looked hurt. "I'm trying to apologize here, Amy. I don't want our friendship to suffer just because I'm dating Ashley."

Amy stopped and stared at him. "You're *dating* her!"

"Yeah," Matt admitted awkwardly. "Look, I know how you feel about Ashley," he said quickly, "but if you were just to spend some time with her…"

"Spend time with Ashley!" Amy exclaimed, all the concern and unhappiness she was feeling bursting out of her as the enormity of his betrayal hit her. "Get real, Matt! I'd rather stick red-hot needles in my eyes."

"Amy…" Matt said, stepping forward.

Amy shook her head. "Look if you want to go out with Ashley, that's fine. You go ahead. Just don't expect me to be friends with her as well." And with that, she swung her backpack on to her shoulder and marched away.

* * *

For the rest of the day, Matt avoided Amy. The sight of Ashley's hand resting possessively on Matt's arm made Amy so annoyed that it squashed any guilt she was feeling about arguing with him when he'd been trying to make friends. She felt completely betrayed. Matt *knew* she couldn't stand Ashley. How could he even think about dating her?

As soon as school finished, she grabbed her books and set off at a run. Marnie was already parked on the road outside the school, ready to take her to the hospital.

"Relax," she said as Amy pulled open the car door. "I rang the hospital before I left. They said it's OK to visit. Your grandpa's not got any worse."

Amy felt a wave of relief rush over her. "Thanks, Marnie," she said. "Has Lou rung?"

Marnie shook her head. "No."

Wondering whether that was good or bad, Amy sat back as Marnie drove through the traffic to the hospital. When they got there, Marnie suggested waiting in the reception area for Amy, in case having two visitors tired Jack out.

Amy went nervously to Grandpa's room on her own. It quickly became clear that his condition hadn't changed. His breathing was short and shallow and every so often he reached for the mask at the side of the bed to get a boost of oxygen to his lungs.

"You don't look too good, Grandpa," Amy said from the doorway, as he coughed painfully.

"The doctor says it's just a small setback," Grandpa wheezed. "Nothing to worry about. Is there any news from Lou?"

Amy shook her head. "Not yet."

"I suppose she'll ring tonight," Grandpa said. He took a deep breath. "Well, tell me about you. And the yard."

Amy sat down next to him and rattled on about the horses, hoping that if she kept talking then Grandpa wouldn't try to. He listened and nodded. "And Marnie's settling in?" he said, as Amy paused for breath.

"Yeah, she's great," Amy said. "She's been helping Ty and Ben today while I've been at school."

"Good," Grandpa said, looking relieved. "So you're all managing?"

"Yes," Amy told him firmly. She squeezed his hand. "You mustn't worry about us, Grandpa. You just think about getting better."

When Amy and Marnie returned to Heartland they found Scott there. "I just dropped in to leave Ty a birthday present for tomorrow," he said as Amy jumped out of the car and ran over to him. "How's your grandpa?"

"Not brilliant," Amy admitted, realizing that she'd totally forgotten it was Ty's birthday the next day. Luckily she'd already got him a present that day she'd been in town.

"Well, send Jack my best wishes," Scott said. "I'll stop by and visit him when he's feeling up to it."

Just then, Marnie came over. "Hi, Scott," she said warmly. "It's nice to see you again."

"You too, Marnie," Scott smiled. He opened the car door to get in but stopped. "So, have you heard from Lou?" he asked casually.

"She rang last night," Amy replied. "Didn't she ring you too?" As soon as the tactless question left her lips, she cursed herself.

Scott's mouth tightened slightly. "No," he said.

"She sounded really tired," Amy stammered quickly. "She'll probably ring you tonight or tomorrow."

"Yeah, whatever," Scott said, but he sounded as if he didn't quite believe her.

Amy suddenly remembered that his reunion was scheduled for the next evening. "Are you still going to the dinner at your old vet school?" she asked.

Scott nodded.

"What's this?" Marnie asked curiously.

Scott explained about the reunion. "It's black tie. All very formal."

"It sounds kind of fun," Marnie said.

"You think?" Scott said.

"Sure," Marnie said. "I love things like that."

Scott frowned. "Hey, you don't fancy coming with me, do you?"

Marnie's eyes widened in surprise. "Come with you?"

"Yeah, I've still got Lou's ticket and if you want to use it you're more than welcome," Scott replied. "It would be lot more fun than going on my own."

"Well, if you're sure," Marnie said, beaming. She turned to Amy. "You'll be all right on your own tomorrow evening, won't you?"

"Of course I will," Amy said. "You go."

Scott smiled at Marnie. "In that case, I'd be honoured if you'll be my partner. I'll pick you up at seven." Then he got into his jeep and drove away.

Marnie looked stunned. "Wow!" she said to Amy. "I wasn't expecting that." She glanced at her watch. "If I'm quick I'll just have time to shoot into town now to find something to wear." She headed back to her car. "I'll catch you later."

"See you," Amy called after her.

As Marnie turned the car round and drove off, Ty came down the yard.

"What's going on?" he asked, in surprise. "Where's Marnie going?"

"Scott's invited her to his vet dinner tomorrow," Amy told him. "So she's gone to buy something to wear."

"So, how was Jack?" Ty asked.

Amy quickly filled him in. "He says it's just a setback, but he didn't look good. It seemed to hurt him to talk – even to breathe." She looked into Ty's familiar, understanding face and suddenly felt the urge to confide the fears she had been having since leaving the hospital, fears that she hadn't even admitted to Marnie. "You know what he's like, Ty, he'll never admit that there's anything wrong. I just hope he's not keeping something from me."

"You didn't see a doctor?" Ty said.

Amy shook her head. "They were all busy."

"Well, make sure you speak to one tomorrow," Ty said.

"I will," Amy sighed. At that moment, the phone rang. "That might be Lou!" she exclaimed.

She ran down to the kitchen. "Heartland — Amy Fleming speaking."

"Hi, Amy, it's me."

"Lou!" Amy sat down with the phone, her heart starting to pound. "How are you? What's happened? Have you seen Daddy?"

"No," Lou said, sounding very disappointed. "I went to the address but it's not Daddy's house, it belongs to some friends of his. A neighbour I spoke to said that the family who live there — the Carters — were away until Saturday. She told me that Daddy had been staying with the Carters for a while but she didn't know where he was now."

"I don't get it," Amy said, confused. "Why did Daddy leave that address at the hotel, then?"

Lou sighed. "I don't know."

"There must be some way of finding out where he is," Amy said, hating to hear Lou sounding so miserable. "Maybe these people, the Carters, will be able to tell you when they get home. I mean, he could have just been staying with them while he had his house fixed up or something."

"I guess," Lou said.

"It only means waiting two more days," Amy told her, trying to cheer her up.

"Yeah, you're right," Lou replied. "I'll find somewhere round here to stay and go and see the Carters on Saturday. So, how's Grandpa?" she asked anxiously.

"He's doing just fine," Amy lied. Lou sounded so down that she couldn't tell her about Grandpa's setback.

"That's good," Lou said. "Is Marnie there? Can I speak to her?"

"Actually, she's out," Amy said.

"Out?" Lou echoed.

Amy hesitated, suddenly wondering how Lou would take the news. "Yes. She's ... um ... gone out shopping for an outfit. Scott's invited her to that dinner tomorrow."

There was a silence on the other end of the line.

"It's just as friends," Amy said quickly, in case Lou was getting the wrong idea. "I mean you know Marnie and Scott would never..."

"I know," Lou broke in. There was a pause. When she spoke again, her voice was flat. "Well, I'd better go. Tell Marnie that I hope she has a good time tomorrow."

"I will," Amy promised.

When Amy walked out of the house, she found Ty waiting on the yard. "Was it Lou?" he asked.

"Yep," Amy said.

"So?" Ty prompted, when she didn't say anything more. "Did she see your father?"

Amy told him what had happened. "She sounded so down," she said to Ty. "I wish I could do something."

"Well, you can't," Ty said gently. His eyes searched hers. "Look, you shouldn't be on your own tomorrow night," he said suddenly. "How about I come over and cook us some supper?"

"On your birthday!" Amy said in surprise. "Don't you want to go out?"

"I can go out any time."

"But..." Amy began.

"No buts," Ty interrupted. "It's decided. I'll stay and keep you company tomorrow night until Marnie gets back."

He looked so determined that Amy gave in. "OK," she smiled gratefully. "Thanks."

Chapter Nine

When Amy woke up the next morning, the air felt strangely silent. Jumping out of bed, she went to the window. It had snowed heavily in the night and the yard and fields were covered in a thick white blanket. Everywhere looked very bleak.

"I'm not going to school today," Amy told Marnie, when she went downstairs. "Now it's snowed there's going to be loads to do on the yard and I don't want to wait until this afternoon to see Grandpa."

Marnie took one look at her determined face and seemed to realize that there was no point in trying to argue. "OK," she said. "I'm not going to force you. But you will go back on Monday, won't you?"

Amy nodded and pulled on her boots. Right now, school just seemed so unimportant, but she guessed she couldn't stay away for ever.

She went outside to give the horses their breakfasts. As she fed Melody, she heard Daybreak cough. She looked carefully at the foal. Daybreak's nose was still running and her eyes looked dull. She checked the foal's temperature. It was normal but Amy made a mental note to ring Scott if the filly had still made no improvement by the following day.

Ty and Ben arrived and they all set to work on the yard. The snow meant that there was a whole heap of extra chores to do — ice in the water troughs to be broken, extra straw to put down on the horses' beds, the yard to be cleared. Amy hurried about, trying not to think about Grandpa and Lou, just trying to keep things going.

When Amy visited Grandpa later, she forced herself to be as cheerful as possible so that he wouldn't worry. "How's the yard?" he wheezed.

"Everything's just fine," Amy told him.

Grandpa looked at her in concern. "You're looking tired, honey."

"Me? No, I'm all right," Amy said, smiling and trying to look wide-awake. "Lou rang last night," she said, changing the subject quickly. "She sent her love."

Jack took a sip of water from the glass by his bedside. "Has she been in touch with your father yet?"

"No, she went to the address but it wasn't Daddy's house," Amy replied. "It just belongs to some friends of his and they're away until Saturday. She's hoping to see them then to find out where he's living."

For a moment Grandpa didn't speak. "I hope she's doing the right thing," he said at last.

Amy decided not to tell him how unhappy Lou had sounded on the phone. "I'm sure she is," she said, wishing she could believe it.

When Amy got back to Heartland, she immediately set back to work. There was something soothing about working. It meant she didn't have to think.

At half-past six, Amy and Ty turned off the lights on the yard and went into the house. They had just got out some cook-books and were arguing about what to eat for supper when Marnie came downstairs. "Well, what do you think?" she demanded, appearing in the doorway.

"You look amazing!" Amy exclaimed.

It was true. Marnie was wearing a long black evening dress. It had a low back and the neckline and straps were intricately beaded with delicate crystals. Her wild blonde hair was caught up in a matching black slide and she was wearing high-heeled strappy shoes.

"Hmm," Ty said. "That's some outfit."

Marnie grinned. "Well, just think of all the hunky young vets who'll be there. I'm planning to have me some fun!"

Just then, Scott beeped his horn outside. "See you later," Marnie said, going to the door.

"Bye!" Ty and Amy called together.

As the door shut behind her, Ty grinned. "I hope they have

a good time. Now," he said, turning back to a cookery book on the kitchen table. "What do you mean you don't like aubergines?"

"I just don't," Amy said. "Can't we have..." she pulled the book away from him, "farmhouse chicken casserole?"

"Too boring," Ty said. He stood up. "No, it looks like I'm just going to have to cook you a Ty special."

"What's in a Ty special?" Amy asked dubiously.

"Aha — you'll have to wait and see," Ty said. "Now, you go upstairs and get changed and I'll get started on the cooking."

"I'm glad it's not your birthday every day — it makes you very bossy," Amy teased, but as she went upstairs she couldn't help feeling glad that he had insisted on staying.

When she came downstairs, Ty was busy frying some bacon.

"What can I do to help?" Amy asked.

"You could peel those potatoes," Ty said, nodding to a bag he'd put on the table. "Then they need slicing." Amy fetched a peeler and a bowl of water and set to work.

As they worked, they chatted about the horses.

"Daybreak's been coughing a bit today," Ty said, after a bit. "And her nose is still running."

"Yeah, I noticed that as well," Amy said. "I thought I might ring Scott tomorrow and get him to take a look at her."

Just then, the phone rang. Amy picked up the receiver.

It was Lou. "How's Grandpa?" she asked.

"He's doing just fine," Amy lied. "How are you?"

Lou sighed. "OK, I suppose." She paused. "It's ... it's just strange, England seems so different." She forced a laugh. "I've always thought of it as my home, but suddenly it doesn't seem like that any more. Maybe it's because it's almost Christmas, but I can't stop thinking about all of you. I'm really missing everyone. I just keep wondering whether coming over here was a big mistake."

Amy heard the unhappiness in her sister's voice. "Of course it wasn't," she said firmly. "You'll meet the Carters tomorrow, they'll tell you where Daddy is and then you'll be able to go and see him. It's all going to be worth it in the end."

"I suppose so," Lou said. She sighed. "Still, right now, I wish I was there with you."

As Amy put the phone down, Ty looked at her. "Trouble?" he asked, looking at her face.

"No. Well, not really," Amy said, sitting down. "Lou's just feeling down." She shook her head. "I wish there was something I could do to help."

Ty looked at her sympathetically. "She'll be back here soon."

Amy nodded. "Yeah."

"Come on, cheer up," Ty said softly. He crouched beside her, taking her hands. "You're taking on everyone's worries at the moment, aren't you?"

Amy looked down into his familiar green eyes and, for a moment, it was as though she was seeing his face for the first time. Her gaze followed the sweep of his cheekbones down to his serious, sensitive mouth. Meeting his eyes again, she saw a warmth there, just like there had been the night of the Grants' party. Feeling herself blush, Amy jumped to her feet, unnerved.

"I haven't given you your birthday present yet," she gabbled. "I'll just get it."

She ran up the stairs, her heart pounding and her palms damp. What was the matter with her?

Reaching her bedroom, she picked up the gift from her dressing-table. Forcing herself to stop, she took a few deep breaths. It was just the stress of everything, she told herself. She was overreacting. All Ty had done was hold her hands. But, as she shut her eyes, an image of his face forced herself into her mind. It was the way his eyes had looked at her – so deep and so searching...

Stop it, she said, catching herself before her crazy thoughts could go any further.

Looking in the mirror, she saw that her cheeks were still flushed. She took another few deep breaths to calm down and then went back downstairs with the gift.

Ty was setting the table. "Here," Amy said, holding out the box and the card she had got him. "There's a card and present from Lou and Grandpa for you as well," she said.

Ty opened the cards first and then Lou and Grandpa's gift – a new riding hat and a pair of gloves.

"Wow," Ty said. "These are great!"

"Now open mine," Amy said, eager to see what he would think of the present she had bought for him.

Ty picked up the package and began to open it. Amy watched his face as he took out her gift – a leather-bound book on herbal remedies for horses signed by the author, George Verrall. She knew Ty had been wanting it for ages and she had got the bookshop in town to order it specially.

"Look inside," she said eagerly as Ty took the book out of the wrapping paper. Below George Verrall's signature, Amy had written her mom's words: *By healing, we heal ourselves.*

"Do you like it?" she asked anxiously, as Ty read the words.

"This is very special," Ty said softly, touching the quotation with his forefinger and looking at her. "Thank you."

As she met his warm gaze, Amy's stomach seemed to turn a somersault. For a moment, the two of them just stared at each other and then Ty stepped forward. Almost before Amy knew what was happening, his arms were folding around her and his lips were moving to meet her own.

Suddenly the phone rang.

Amy and Ty broke apart. Blushing to her hair roots, Amy darted over the kitchen and grabbed the handset. "Heartland," she stammered. "Amy Fleming speaking."

An efficient voice spoke on the other end. "Hello, Amy, this is Dr Marshall from Meadowville Park Hospital.

Amy's heart skipped a beat. "Dr Marshall," she echoed. "Is it Grandpa? Is he all right?"

There was a slight pause. "I'm afraid I've got some bad news," Dr Marshall said gently.

Amy felt her insides turn to ice. "What is it?"

"Your grandfather's condition has deteriorated in the last few hours," Dr Marshall replied. "One of his lungs has collapsed. He's in Intensive Care. I think you had better come to the hospital straight away."

Chapter Ten

Ty was beside Amy even before she had put the phone down. "Was that the hospital?" he demanded. "What's wrong?"

Amy started to shake. "It's Grandpa," she whispered, so distraught that she could barely get the words out. "He's been moved to Intensive Care. I've got to go to the hospital."

Not stopping to ask any more questions, Ty grabbed their coats from the back of the door. "Come on," he said, shoving her jacket into her arms. "I'll drive you."

Moving automatically, Amy pulled her jacket on. "What about Marnie?" she said suddenly. "She'll wonder where we are."

"I'll leave her a note to tell her we've gone to the hospital," Ty said. He tore a piece of paper from the notebook by the phone and scribbled a message. He left it in a prominent position on the table and turned off the oven. "Let's go."

Too scared to think straight, Amy followed him out of the house. A light snow was falling but she hardly even noticed as the flakes caught in her hair. She got into the pick-up and huddled against the cold seat. Ty turned the key and the engine belched into life.

"So, what did the hospital say?" Ty asked, swinging the truck round and setting off down the driveway.

"One of Grandpa's lungs has collapsed." Amy's teeth began to chatter.

Ty looked at her in concern. "Here," he said, pulling a travel rug out from beneath the seat and tossing it to her. "You're in shock."

Amy wrapped the rug around herself but neither it nor the roaring fan heater could stop her from shivering. At the first set of traffic-lights, Ty stopped, rummaged in the glove compartment, and pulled out a small brown bottle with a dropper in the top. "Bach Flower Rescue Remedy," he said softly, handing it to her. "Take four drops under your tongue. Keep taking them every ten minutes till we get to the hospital."

Blindly, Amy did what he said. All she could think about was Grandpa. A collapsed lung! What if he didn't get better? What if he ... died?

Oh, please, she prayed desperately as the wheels of the truck cut through the slush on the roads and the lights of the late-night shops flashed past. *I'll do anything. Just please don't let Grandpa die!*

The half-hour journey to the hospital seemed to take for ever, but at last Ty pulled up in the empty visitors' car park outside the sprawling complex of low white buildings. Once in the hospital, they were shown into a small room where, a few minutes later, Dr Marshall joined them.

"How's my grandpa?" Amy asked, jumping to her feet.

"His condition's very serious," Dr Marshall said gravely.

"Will he die?" Amy whispered.

"Collapsed lungs aren't usually life-threatening providing treatment is administered quickly," Dr Marshall replied. "However, in your grandfather's case there have been complications."

"Complications?" Amy echoed.

"He has what is known as a tension pnemothorax, which means that the air can't escape from his good lung," Dr Marshall explained. "It's a potentially fatal condition. Now, that doesn't mean he's going to die," she added quickly, seeing Amy's face. "We've stabilized his condition. However, I have to tell you that the next few hours will be critical."

"Can I see him?" Amy asked, hardly able to get the words out, she was so worried.

Dr Marshall nodded. "He's sedated at the moment but yes, you can see him."

Amy and Ty followed the doctor down the corridors.

When they reached the Intensive Care Unit, Dr Marshall opened the door.

Poor Grandpa was lying immobile on the hospital bed, his eyes shut. Tubes led into his nose, chest and wrist and beside the bed several machines blinked and whirred. A nurse was bustling around. Seeing Amy, she looked at her sympathetically. "Are you Mr Bartlett's grand-daughter?"

Amy nodded, her eyes on the still figure in the bed. She felt Ty's hand squeeze her shoulder and, as the nurse moved out of the way, she went over to the bed. Grandpa's skin was very pale and his hands lay still on the bedclothes.

Swallowing hard, Amy sat down on the chair beside the bed and put her hand over one of Grandpa's. It was cold and clammy.

"We'll leave you for a few moments," Dr Marshall said. "If there's any problem, just press the red button on the wall."

The door shut behind the doctor and nurse.

"Do you want me to stay or would you rather be on your own?" Ty asked softly.

Amy looked up at him. "Stay – please." She turned to Grandpa again. "Ty, I just can't bear to see him like this."

Ty put his arm around her shoulders. "Hang on, Amy. It'll be OK."

"First Mom and then Pegasus and now..." She bit her lip, struggling not to give way to the anguish that was threatening to overwhelm her. She bent her head, her long hair falling across her face. "I love him so much."

"And he loves you, Amy," Ty said, crouching beside her, his eyes intense. "Come on, you know what your grandpa's like. He won't give up. He's a fighter."

Amy swallowed, knowing Ty was right. "Grandpa, can you hear me?" she whispered, clutching her grandfather's limp hand. "You've got to fight – please, *fight*."

The long hours of the night passed slowly. Amy hardly moved from Grandpa's bedside. Just after two o'clock in the morning, Scott and Marnie appeared at the door of the Intensive Care Unit.

"Amy," Marnie whispered. "We came as soon as we saw the note."

Pulling away from Grandpa, she went to the doorway and hugged them both.

"Does Lou know?" Scott asked.

Amy shook her head bleakly. "I don't know where she's staying tonight."

Scott cursed under his breath.

Amy glanced at the door. She didn't want to be away from Grandpa for even a second. "I'm going back in."

Leaving Ty to explain exactly what had happened, she returned to Grandpa's side.

After ten minutes, Ty returned. "Marnie's offered to stay here with you," he said. "I'm going to go back to Heartland so that I can see to the horses in the morning. Ben will need to be told as well. Is that OK?"

Amy nodded. She didn't want Ty to go, but she knew that his suggestion made sense. Marnie didn't know enough about the horses to see to them herself and Ty was right — Ben needed to know what was going on.

"It'll mean someone's there if Lou calls, as well," Ty said. "You'll be all right with Marnie, won't you?"

"Yeah," Amy said. She forced her lips into a smile and stood up. "Thanks, Ty."

"No problem," Ty said. "Just remember — don't give up." He hugged her for a moment, then left.

Marnie sat with Amy through the remainder of that long night. They talked a little but mainly sat without speaking as the hours ticked by. Amy was glad of the silence. Her mind felt as if it had shut down, as if all normal actions — like speaking and smiling — were beyond her. All she wanted was for Grandpa to open his eyes and speak to her, to show her that he was going to get better.

She remembered the hours she had spent with him when she had been too little to help her mom on the yard — helping him clean the house, weed the vegetable garden, do the shopping. All the games he'd played with her. She remembered how he had always been there for her — when Mom was too busy. Grandpa had been the one who listened when she wanted to talk, who helped her with her school projects.

As she looked at his lined face lying against the pillow, she realized that he had grown older without her noticing. He had always had such energy that she had never really thought of him as old, but now her gaze traced the deep grooves on his forehead, the wrinkles around his eyes. She and Lou should have insisted that he took things easier.

As the grey light of dawn streaked across the dark sky, she put a hand to his face and imagined what life would be like without him. "Grandpa," she whispered. "I love you."

Her hand froze. His eyelids had moved. Had she imagined it?

"Grandpa?" she said.

This time she knew there was no mistake. Grandpa blinked. His lips moved but his voice barely made a sound. "Amy?"

"Yes, Grandpa!" Amy gasped. "It's me!"

Behind her, she heard Marnie jump to her feet. "I'll get a doctor."

Amy barely registered the sound of the door opening and shutting. Grandpa's eyes blinked open again. "Throat's dry ... water..." he croaked.

"The doctor will be here in a minute," Amy told him, clutching his hand, silently praying that Grandpa was now going to be OK.

Over the next half hour, a succession of doctors and nurses hurried in and out of Jack's room, until, at last, Amy was left alone with him again. He was still attached to all the tubes and his face was still pale, but at least he was awake.

Amy kissed him gently on the cheek. "I was so worried about you, Grandpa," she said.

Jack spoke slowly, every breath an effort. "It'll take more than a bit of pneumonia to get rid of me," he whispered. He covered her hand with his. "You look tired, honey. What time is it?"

"It's early in the morning. I've been here all night but I'm OK."

"Lou…" Jack began.

"As soon as she rings I'll tell her what's happened," Amy said quickly. "She'll get back in no time, Grandpa."

"No!" Grandpa wheezed. "Don't worry her. I don't want her to come back just for me… Make her stay where she is until she's seen your father."

"But Grandpa," Amy began. "She'll want to be here. She'll…"

"No, Amy," Jack insisted weakly. "I stopped her seeing your father before, I'm not going to be the one to stop her again… Please, promise me … you'll make her stay."

Amy stared at him. How *could* she promise that? But then, she couldn't bear to see the distress in Grandpa's eyes. "I'll try," she agreed reluctantly.

"Thank you," Grandpa said, the words no more than a whisper as he sank back against the pillows.

"I'd better go," Amy said. "But I'll be back later. You get some rest now, Grandpa."

He nodded and closed his eyes. Amy heard a sigh of relief as he drifted off to sleep.

Amy followed Marnie out of the hospital and into the car park. It had stopped snowing now, but the heavy morning clouds overhead seemed to promise that there was more to come. The freezing air hit Amy's face like a splash of icy water but, instead of making her feel more awake, it seemed to have the opposite effect. The adrenalin that had been surging through her body over the last fourteen hours suddenly drained out of her and all her muscles turned to lead. Getting into Marnie's car, she leant her head heavily against the window.

"I think it's bed for us when we get back," Marnie said, starting the engine.

As Marnie drove home, Amy blinked hard to stop her eyes from shutting. She looked at Marnie. Her blonde curls had long since escaped from their slide and her evening dress was creased and rumpled. "Thanks for staying with me, Marnie," Amy said gratefully.

Marnie turned her tired eyes to her and smiled. "That's what friends are for. I couldn't have left you there on your own." She yawned. "I'm just glad Jack's getting better."

When they reached Heartland, Ty and Ben came hurrying down the yard to meet them.

"How's Jack?" Ty asked.

"Still improving," Marnie said.

Amy noticed the dark shadows beneath Ty's eyes. He looked as if he'd hardly slept. "Has Lou rung?" she asked.

Ty shook his head.

"Come on," Ben said, leading the way to the house. "We've got some coffee on and you both look like you could use something to eat."

They followed him into the house. Once in the kitchen, Amy sank down on a chair at the table and let her head rest on her arms.

Her mind was just starting to swim towards sleep when she felt Marnie's hand on her shoulder. "Go to bed," Marnie said gently. "You can eat later. Right now you need to rest."

Amy fell into bed and slept for six straight hours. When she woke up, daylight was streaming in through her window. She looked around in confusion. What was she doing in bed? Gradually the events of the last twenty-four hours came rolling back. Grandpa. The hospital...

Jumping out of bed, she went downstairs. The kitchen was deserted. She picked up the phone and called the hospital. Dr Marshall had gone off duty but one of her colleagues came to the phone to speak to Amy.

"Your grandfather's doing well," he said reassuringly. "His lung has stabilized and, providing all goes well, the damage should now start to heal. We'll need to monitor his condition very carefully over the next week. In this sort of case, there's always the danger that the lung could collapse again.

If that happened, then we'd be looking at major surgery. However, such relapses are rare and we're hopeful that your grandfather will make a rapid and full recovery."

Feeling comforted by the doctor's words, Amy replaced the receiver. As she did so, her gaze fell on Ty's birthday presents. They had been piled up on the dresser, forgotten in the drama of the night before. The sight of them brought a vivid memory flashing into Amy's mind — Ty's arms wrapping around her, his lips lowering to meet her own…

The back door opened. Amy jumped and swung round. It was Ty.

"Ty," Amy stammered, acutely aware of what she'd just been thinking.

Ty didn't seem to notice her confusion. "I was just coming in to leave you a note," he said, rubbing a weary hand across his eyes. "Ben's offered to finish off the horses so I thought I'd crash out for a while at home. If that's OK?"

"Of course," Amy said. "You must be exhausted."

Ty forced a smile. "I'll live. Is there any news on Jack?"

"I've just spoken to the hospital." Amy told him what the doctor had said. "He sounded pleased with Grandpa's progress," she finished.

"Good," Ty said, looking relieved. "Well, I'll see you tomorrow, then."

"Don't forget your birthday presents," Amy said quickly, as he turned to go.

Ty glanced at the dresser and then his eyes swung swiftly

to hers. From the suddenly guarded look on his face, Amy was sure that he too was remembering the night before. She caught her breath, thinking that he was about to say something. But then, in a split second, he seemed to change his mind and the tension left his face.

"Thanks for reminding me," he said, going to the dresser and gathering up his gifts. When he turned to Amy again, his eyes showed nothing more than friendly concern. "Look, if you need me for anything, just give me a call."

Not trusting herself to speak, Amy nodded.

As the door closed behind him, she sank down on a chair, feeling confused and mixed-up. Her thoughts whirled. There was so much to think about. Grandpa, Ty... She put her head in her hands. It was all getting too much.

Hearing footsteps on the stairs, she looked up as Marnie came into the kitchen. "I thought I heard you down here," Marnie said, yawning. "Is there any news from the hospital?"

Quickly pulling herself together, Amy filled Marnie in on her conversation with the doctor. Just as she was finishing, the phone rang.

"Hi, Amy." It was Lou. Her voice sounded shaky.

"Lou!" Amy exclaimed, glancing at Marnie in relief. "Am I glad you've called. It's..." But before she could finish, Lou broke in.

"Oh, Amy," she said, bursting into tears.

For a second, Amy was almost too shocked to speak. Lou never cried. "Lou!" she said in alarm. "What's happened?"

"It's Daddy." Lou sobbed.

Horrible thoughts raced through Amy's mind. Daddy! Was he injured? Dead? "What's the matter?" she said quickly. "He's not..."

"No," Lou said, seeming to read her thoughts. "He's OK. It's just ... just ... he's not here. He's in Australia."

"Australia!" Amy echoed, astounded. "What's he doing there?"

"He lives there," Lou said.

Amy began to feel that she was losing her grip on the conversation. "What do you mean?"

"I went to see the Carters today," Lou explained, sounding like she was struggling to control herself. "Michael Carter is not just friends with Daddy, he's his business partner as well. They have a company that specializes in importing and exporting horses from England to Australia. He told me that when Daddy's over here he stays with them, but that he actually lives in Australia."

"But Daddy never mentioned living in Australia in his letter," Amy said, trying to get her head round what Lou was saying.

"I can't believe I've come all this way for nothing," Lou said.

Amy didn't know what to say. She understood the disappointment Lou must be feeling — to have psyched herself up for meeting their father, only to find he wasn't even there.

"You'll get to see him soon," Amy said, trying to comfort her.

"But I've been so stupid," Lou sniffed. "I should never have left Heartland. Particularly with Grandpa being ill and everything. How is he today?"

Amy paused. The last thing she wanted was to make Lou's unhappiness worse but she knew she had to tell her the truth. "Um ... he's not good, Lou," she said. She took a deep breath. "One of his lungs collapsed last night."

Lou gasped. Amy quickly explained what had happened.

"What am I going to do?" Lou said in an anguished voice. "I need to be with him straight away. I'm coming home," Lou said determinedly. "I'm going to go and change my flight tomorrow – get the first seat out I can." She swallowed hard. "Tell Grandpa I love him, Amy."

When Amy replaced the receiver, she stood by the phone feeling stunned.

"What's the news?" Marnie asked her anxiously

Amy told her.

"Poor Lou," Marnie said, aghast.

"I wish she was here, Marnie," Amy said.

Marnie put an arm round her shoulders. "Don't worry," she said, hugging her. "She'll be back soon."

After supper, Amy and Marnie returned to the hospital. Grandpa was awake when they arrived. He was still connected to the various tubes and machines, but Amy was relieved to see that some colour had returned to his face. She decided to keep the truth about Lou and Daddy for when he had recovered some more.

When Amy and Marnie got back to Heartland, Marnie announced that she was going to go to bed. "You look like you could use some sleep too," she said to Amy.

But Amy's mind was buzzing with thoughts of Grandpa, Lou and Daddy. "I think I'll stay up for a bit," she said, sitting down in an armchair and picking up the remote control. "I'll watch TV."

"Do you want some company?" Marnie asked her.

Amy shook her head. "No, I'll be fine. You go to bed."

"Night, then," Marnie said and she went upstairs.

Amy flicked through the channels and eventually settled on watching a trashy sit-com. By ten-thirty she was almost asleep in the chair. Yawning widely, she got to her feet and turned the TV off. She went to the kitchen window. Apart from the lights on the front stable block everywhere was dark. She was about to go upstairs to bed when she hesitated. For some reason, she felt that something wasn't right. She glanced outside again. Everything seemed quiet enough but still she felt a nagging urge to go and check.

With a sigh, she pulled on her jacket and boots. She was probably worrying about nothing, but she knew she wouldn't be able to relax until she had looked around the yard and checked that everything really was OK.

She went out into the darkness. As she walked up the yard

she thought about Lou. She hoped her sister could get an early flight. It would be wonderful to have her home again.

The top doors of the stalls in the stable block were all shut. Amy opened each one and checked inside but all the horses appeared to be happy and content.

She turned and trudged through the snow to the back barn. Pulling back the door, she slipped inside and pressed the light-switch. There were a few startled snorts from the stalls as the lights flickered on but no sounds of distress from any of the stalls. Still, Amy walked down the aisle, checking over each stall door. Dancer, Sundance, Jasmine...

She reached Daybreak and Melody's stall. The mare was pulling at her hay net and the little filly was standing beside her. Amy was about to pass on to the next stall when she paused. Daybreak was standing unusually still, her sides moving in and out.

Feeling a sudden prickle of worry run down her spine, Amy pushed back the bolt on the door. Melody looked round but Daybreak didn't. Lowering her head, the foal coughed. Amy went over to her and, for once, Daybreak didn't try and move away. She stood submissively as Amy gently felt her glands. They were swollen. With mounting concern, Amy noticed that the filly had a thick yellow discharge running from her nose and that her eyes were dull. There was no doubt about it, Daybreak was ill – possibly very ill.

Chapter Eleven

"Equine Herpesvirus," Scott said an hour later, as he stepped back from examining Daybreak, "I'm sure of it." He patted the foal. "Though I'll need to run a few tests to confirm it."

"What does that mean?" Marnie asked, from the doorway.

"It's a virus that causes respiratory infection," Scott replied. While Amy held Daybreak, he took a blood sample and a sample of mucus from the foal's windpipe. "It particularly affects young horses," he went on. "At first the symptoms are mild – a clear nasal discharge, occasional cough and possibly a rise in temperature. It doesn't look too serious but, if left untreated, a more serious secondary bacterial infection can occur. That's what's happened to Daybreak."

"But how would she have got it?" Amy asked.

"I imagine one of the other horses must have brought it

on to the yard," Scott said. "It generally doesn't affect adult horses so badly, so you probably haven't noticed it. Daybreak's been affected more severely because at her age she still has a relatively immature immune system." He looked at Amy. "Have you noticed her nose running in the last week or so?"

"Yes," Amy said, feeling horribly guilty. "I was going to call you yesterday but then, with Grandpa at the hospital, I just forgot."

Scott nodded sympathetically. "That's understandable. You've had a lot on. Well, don't worry. I think we've caught it early enough. Daybreak will need a course of antibiotics to control the secondary infection and some mucolytic drugs to liquidize the mucus in her lungs. Nursing is also very important if she's to recover quickly. She needs warmth, rest – just short lead-walks each day – and she needs to avoid dust. It might be better to move her and Melody to one of the front stables in the morning so she can easily get fresh air. Keep the bedding deep and clean and try and watch to see if she keeps feeding. I'll call in tomorrow and vaccinate the other horses to stop the virus spreading any further."

"Can I use any herbs to help Daybreak?" Amy asked.

Scott nodded. "Anything that will help her expel the mucus is ideal – you might want to try eucalyptus or tea-tree oil."

He rummaged in his bag and took out a syringe and a bottle of antibiotics. After shaking the bottle, he filled the syringe and injected the antibiotics into Daybreak's hind-quarters. "OK," he said. "I'll come back tomorrow morning and see how she's getting on."

It was gone midnight when Scott left and Amy went into the tack-room. Near the medicine cabinet was a shelf of books that had once belonged to her mom. She picked one on herbal remedies and began to leaf through the pages.

"You're not going to do anything more tonight, are you?" Marnie said, coming into the tack-room.

Amy looked up. "I want to see if I can find anything to help her."

"But Amy, you're exhausted," Marnie said.

"I'm OK," Amy replied. She did feel incredibly tired, but she also felt incredibly guilty. How could she have forgotten about calling Scott? If she'd got him out a few days ago, maybe Daybreak wouldn't be so ill now. She saw Marnie's worried face. "I won't stay out long – I promise," she said. "But I'm not coming in just yet."

Her voice was so determined that Marnie had no choice but to give in. "All right," she said reluctantly. "But I'll make you some hot chocolate to keep you going."

Alone in the tack-room, Amy ran her eyes over the pages on respiratory infections and herbal expectorants. Although garlic was highly recommended, the book suggested that it could upset the digestive system of young foals so she decided to use echinacea roots instead. Echinacea, she read, had excellent antiviral and antibacterial qualities. It would stimulate the body to produce more white blood cells to fight the infection and it could safely be used with antibiotics. She checked the dosage – ten grams of the cut root a day – and took some out of the cabinet. She also took out a bottle of eucalyptus oil and some cotton wool before returning to Daybreak's stall.

The little filly was still standing dejectedly beside Melody. Her head was hanging and her nose streamed. Her ears barely flickered as Amy looked over the door.

"It's all right," Amy told her softly. "You'll soon get better."

Marnie appeared with the hot drink for Amy and helped her fetch a muck skip and some fresh straw to make the bed clean and deep, like Scott had suggested. Once the stall had been cleared and the new straw added, Amy crouched down beside Daybreak's head and encouraged her to eat the cut-up pieces of echinacea root. At first, the filly simply mouthed it with her lips but, as she got the taste of the plant, she began to nibble on the pieces with more interest. It was almost as if she sensed they would help her.

When all the root was gone, Amy wiped Daybreak's nostrils with some clean cotton wool and then poured a few drops of eucalyptus oil on to a fresh piece of cotton wool. Keeping the pad a few centimetres away from Daybreak's nostrils, in case the concentrated oil irritated the foal's skin, Amy let Daybreak inhale the strong scent. She knew eucalyptus oil was supposed to be good for clearing blocked airways and encouraging any infected mucus to be expelled.

After a few minutes, she decided that Daybreak had inhaled enough and took the cotton wool away. As she took it over to the door, Daybreak lay down heavily in the straw. Amy went over and knelt beside the filly. "You're going to be OK," she murmured, stroking Daybreak's neck.

At her touch, the filly lifted her head slightly, a hint of her old spirit in her eyes, but she was too ill to really object. With a cough, she let her muzzle sink back heavily on to the straw. Amy looked at her for a long moment and then crept out of the stall.

As soon as Amy got up the next morning, she pulled on her clothes and went straight to the barn, her head feeling dizzy from lack of sleep. Dawn had hardly broken yet and the freezing wind whipped her face. Winter was really closing in. The turn-out paddocks looked bleak and cold, the thick layer of snow seeming to suffocate the ground.

"How are you, girl?" Amy said, her gloved fingers fumbling with the bolt on the stall door.

The little foal was standing beside her mother. Her breathing was just as fast as it had been the night before and her eyes were dull. She didn't look any better. Amy's heart sank. "We'd better get you cleaned up," she said, looking at the foal's streaming nose.

The other horses in the barn had seen Amy and had

started to kick their doors and call expectantly for their breakfast. But for once Amy ignored them. She fetched some cotton wool and warm water and bathed Daybreak's nostrils, then dried them thoroughly before once again offering the foal some eucalyptus oil to sniff. Daybreak inhaled listlessly, her ears drooping. All the spirit seemed to have been drained out of her.

When Ty and Ben arrived, she told them about Daybreak. Ty looked guilt-stricken. "I can't believe I didn't realize," he said. "I knew she was off-colour. I should have kept a closer eye on her."

"No, it's my fault," Ben said. "You've both been so frantic."

"But that's no excuse!" Ty exclaimed. "I should have seen that Daybreak was seriously ill and called Scott."

Although Amy still felt guilty herself, she was too tired to waste energy on apportioning blame. "Look," she said wearily. "None of us noticed. Let's just leave it at that. Now we just need to try and get her better." She told them what Scott had said.

"She can have Red's stall," Ben offered immediately, heading for the door. "It's the biggest. I'll go and get started on cleaning out his bed."

"Thanks, Ben," Amy said gratefully.

Ty was still angry with himself. "I can't believe I didn't notice," he burst out as Ben left.

Amy sighed. "Ty, don't be so tough on yourself."

Ty looked at her. "But I should be making things easier for you."

Amy looked at him, too tired to smile. "You are," she said.

Amy and Ty took it in turns to monitor the little filly until Scott arrived. He gave her another shot of antibiotics. "Her temperature's still too high," he told them. "Is she feeding?"

Amy nodded. Daybreak wasn't feeding very hard or for very long but she was indeed still suckling.

Scott looked relieved. "Good. Let me know immediately if she stops. It's vital that she keeps feeding. If she doesn't, she'll become dehydrated very quickly."

"We'll keep an eye on her," Ty said.

Amy told Scott about the remedies she had been using. "Keep going," Scott said. "We need to do whatever we can to help her to fight off this infection as quickly as possible." He picked up his bag. "OK, let's go and vaccinate the other horses."

Amy spent the rest of the day with the filly, only leaving her to go and visit Grandpa in hospital. Although the tube to his nose had been removed, a drip still ran into his arm and the chest tubes were still in place. He had seemed a bit brighter but had told her that the doctors didn't think he would be able to leave hospital for another two weeks.

"But that means you'll be in here for Christmas," Amy said, aghast.

"I'm afraid so, honey," Grandpa replied. "But you'll have Lou and Marnie for company and you can come and visit." He squeezed her hand. "It won't be that bad."

It will! Amy wanted to cry, but she saw the worry on Grandpa's face and instead smiled as cheerfully as she could. "No, we'll manage," she said.

But in the car on the way back to Heartland, she felt a tide of emotion threaten to overwhelm her. Her first Christmas without Mom and now she wouldn't have Grandpa either. *Oh, Lou*, she thought desperately, looking out of the car window, tears stinging the back of her eyes, *please hurry home*.

When Lou rang that evening, she had bad news. "I tried to get a flight but I couldn't," she told Amy. "The air-traffic controllers over here are on strike and it doesn't look like I'll be able to get back for a couple more days."

"But you have to!" Amy burst out, feeling a hard lump pressing in her throat. "Lou! I…" she caught the words *need you* just before they left her lips. Lou was upset enough already; she didn't need to be made to feel any worse. "Well, I guess it's only a few more days," she said, forcing herself to sound calm.

"But I don't want to wait. I want to come home."

"You will do soon," Amy said, as brightly as she could.

The second she put the phone down, though, the brightness faded from her face and a wave of bleak misery engulfed her. She couldn't bear it.

A floorboard on the landing above creaked. Guessing that Marnie was coming down, Amy grabbed her jacket and ran outside. She simply couldn't pretend to be strong and cheerful for one second longer.

She ran to the front stable block, her breath coming in short bursts. She unbolted the door of Melody and Daybreak's new stall and went in, collapsed on the straw in the corner and burst into tears.

She looked towards Daybreak lying beside Melody, her head resting on the straw, her breathing noisy. Amy remembered the night the filly had been born. Life had seemed so full of hope then.

"Amy?"

Amy jumped and looked up. Marnie was standing in the doorway of the stall, a horrified look in her eyes as she took in Amy's distraught face. "Amy, what's wrong?" She came over and knelt beside Amy. "What's happened?"

Amy knew that there was no way she could hide the truth from Marnie. "It's Lou," she cried. "And Grandpa and Daybreak and everything! I just can't cope any more."

Marnie put her arms around her. "It's all right," she said soothingly. "I'm here. You don't have to. Now, tell me what's wrong – what's happened with Lou?"

"She can't get home," Amy said and she told Marnie all about Lou's phone call. "She's so unhappy and there's nothing I can do to help her. I'm useless."

Marnie hugged her fiercely. "Amy, you've been wonderful,"

she said. "I've seen how cheerful you've been with your grandpa and how you've been trying so hard not to worry Lou. You've kept things going and it's taken real courage." She shook her head. "I tell you, there's been such a big change in you since I was last here."

Amy looked up at her. "Really?" she asked, surprised at the statement.

"Really," Marnie said softly, her blue eyes searching Amy's face. "Your mom would have been proud of you, Amy. I know she would."

For a moment neither of them spoke.

"Look," Marnie said softly. "Don't worry about Christmas. We'll spend it with your Grandpa in hospital and, if Lou's still in England, we'll ring her every hour if it makes you happier. Don't worry about Daybreak, either. She's going to get better – it'll just take a little while for the medicine and herbs to work, just like it did with your grandpa." She squeezed Amy's arm. "Things will turn out OK, you'll see."

Amy nodded slowly.

Marnie hugged her again. "Come on, let's go back inside."

Amy hesitated. "I will," she said. "In a moment."

Marnie studied her face and then stood up. "OK," she said, seeming to sense Amy's need to be on her own. "But don't stay out here too long."

As Marnie's footsteps faded away, Amy leant back against the stall wall. *Would Mom have been proud of me?* she wondered wearily. *I just don't know.*

She looked at Daybreak lying in the straw, her sides heaving painfully in and out. Amy got to her feet and went over to her. Crouching down, she laid her hand on Daybreak's neck. Resentment flared in the filly's eyes and she threw her head up, but the sudden movement made her cough painfully. With a heavy sigh, she let her muzzle sink back on the straw.

Amy began to massage the foal's neck with slow circular movements. As she felt Daybreak's muscles start to relax she let her hands work up over the foal's neck and then, with a lighter pressure, over her delicate ears, face and nose. Closing her own eyes, she focused completely on the instinctive movement of her fingers. As she breathed in the warm scent of horse and straw, the stress and tension of the last few days seemed to fade away. The world seemed to shrink until it contained nothing but her fingers and Daybreak's skin.

She wasn't sure how long she worked on the little filly but, when she finally opened her eyes, she found that a feeling of peace had crept over her. She glanced at the foal's sides. Daybreak's breathing had slowed; the tension around her muzzle had relaxed. Her eyes were half-shut.

Amy gently eased backwards and stood up, her heart turning over as she looked at the little foal lying so still in the straw. With one last glance at Daybreak, she crept quietly out of the stall.

Chapter Twelve

Amy slept better that night. Although the things she had been worried about the evening before hadn't changed, the time in the stall with Daybreak had somehow calmed her and she awoke conscious of a new feeling of strength. *I can cope*, she thought. *Christmas might not be so good, but Grandpa and Daybreak will get better and Lou will be home sometime soon — I know she will.*

Downstairs, she found Marnie in the kitchen putting on some fresh coffee. "How are you feeling?" she asked.

"Good," Amy replied and, rather than it being just something she said automatically, she found that she really meant it. She smiled. "Yeah, I'm feeling good."

The first thing Amy did when she went out on to the yard was to go to Daybreak and Melody's stall.

The little foal was still lying in the straw, but even from the door Amy could see that her breathing looked calmer. She went into the stall and crouched beside the filly. "Hi, little one," she said, reaching out to gently scratch Daybreak's neck.

At the touch of her hand, the foal lifted her head – but for once her eyes didn't fill with hostility. She stared at Amy for a moment and then turned her head and sniffed the back of Amy's hand. Amy felt a flicker of surprise. "Good girl," she said, tickling Daybreak's muzzle.

As she did so, she noticed that the filly's eyes were brighter. Maybe she was finally beginning to get better.

Feeling much happier, Amy left the stall and went to get the feeds.

She had just finished feeding when Scott's jeep came bumping up the drive. As he parked, Amy saw that he wasn't alone – Matt was with him.

"Hi," Scott said to Amy and Marnie as he and Matt jumped out of the jeep. "How's the patient today?"

"A bit better, I think," Amy said.

"Good," Scott said. "That's what I want to hear."

As Scott got his bag from the back seat, Amy looked uncertainly at Matt. "Hello, Matt."

He smiled awkwardly. "Hi," he said. "Scott's giving me a ride to school. How are you?"

"OK, thanks," Amy replied.

There was a silence. The angry words they had exchanged the last time they'd met trembled in the air between them.

Scott walked over to them. "Should we go and see Daybreak, then?" he said. Not waiting for an answer, he headed up the yard. Marnie shot a curious look at Amy and Matt and then joined him.

Amy was about to follow when Matt caught hold of her arm. "Amy…" he said.

Amy stopped and looked at him.

"I really am sorry," Matt said. "About your grandpa and Daybreak and … and about the argument we had."

Amy nodded.

"Can't we make it up?" Matt continued. "I don't want us to argue about who I'm dating. We've been friends for too long."

"But why *Ashley*?" The words burst out of Amy. "I mean, of all the people in the world, Matt, why her?"

"I like her," Matt said simply. "Since Jade's been going out with Dan I've really got to know her better."

Amy raised her eyebrows sarcastically. "How nice for you."

Matt sighed. "Look, this isn't getting us anywhere." He looked at her. "I might be dating Ashley but you're still one of my best friends, Amy. Don't ask me to choose between you – please."

Amy wavered. She hated the thought of Matt dating Ashley but she couldn't bear the thought of losing him as a friend. "OK," she said at last. "I guess it really isn't my business who you go out with."

"So we're friends again?" Matt smiled.

Amy nodded. "Friends." She managed a teasing smile. "Even if you do have awful taste in girlfriends."

"Well, I did ask *you* out, didn't I?" Matt grinned.

Amy punched his arm and they carried on up the yard.

When they reached Daybreak and Melody's stall they found the foal standing up, suckling vigorously. Scott and Marnie were watching.

"Hey, girl," Amy said, going into the stall.

"She's feeding well – that's a good sign," Scott said.

Amy held the filly still while Scott checked her over.

"Yes, she's definitely on the mend," he said at last as he folded up his stethoscope. "Her breathing's improved, her temperature's almost back to normal and her glands aren't as swollen. I think we can safely say she's over the worst."

Amy breathed out deeply in relief.

"Now, keep up the treatments and the nursing," Scott said. He glanced out of the door. "She needs as much fresh air as possible. The wind's dropped, so you can take her and Melody out for a gentle walk on the lead, but don't turn them out in the field until the weather improves. She's OK to go out in the snow for a while if it's sunny but she mustn't be exposed to wind or rain at the moment. She needs to be kept warm and dry."

"Sure," Amy nodded.

Scott smiled at her. "You're doing a great job, Amy. Daybreak's very lucky to have you around."

Amy felt embarrassed by his words of praise. As they all

walked back down the yard together, she changed the subject. "Has Lou rung you yet?" she asked Scott, as they reached the jeep.

Scott nodded. "She rang last night. She was pretty upset about your dad and everything."

"I know," Amy agreed. "I just hope she gets home soon."

Scott was silent for a moment. "Me too," he said at last, and climbed into the driver's seat.

"See you, Amy," Matt said, opening the passenger door and getting in.

"Yeah, see you," Amy said. "Say hi to Soraya for me and tell her I'll ring her tonight."

She felt hopeful as she watched Scott drive off. Lou must have apologized when she'd called him, mustn't she? She hadn't liked to ask. She knew her sister, and Lou was very strong – and also *very* stubborn. But Amy was certain she was missing Scott, or she wouldn't have phoned him. *Perhaps they've made up after all*, she thought.

Ty came down the yard. "So, what did Scott say about Daybreak?"

"He's really pleased with her progress," Amy said. "He said we should walk her and Melody out on the yard this afternoon."

Ty raised his eyebrows. "That'll be fun."

"She was getting a bit better at leading before she was ill," Amy said hopefully. "She might not be that bad."

Ty didn't look convinced.

* * *

"So, how are all the horses?" Grandpa asked when Amy and Marnie visited him at lunchtime.

"OK," Amy said, glad to be able to tell the truth for once.

"What about Lou?" Grandpa asked. "Has she seen your father yet?"

Amy hesitated. All the tubes and drips had been removed from Grandpa's body and he was starting to look much better. She decided to tell him the truth. "No," she said. "It turns out that he's living in Australia."

"In Australia?" Grandpa echoed.

Amy nodded and told him everything.

"Oh, poor Lou," Grandpa said, as she finished. "She must be so disappointed."

"She is," Amy said quietly.

"So when's she coming home?" Grandpa asked.

"As soon as possible," Amy replied. "There's a strike on at the airport but she's going to get the first flight back that she can."

Grandpa looked worried. "I hope she's back in time for Christmas."

"I know," Amy said.

That afternoon, Amy fetched Melody's and Daybreak's halters. "Now, be good," she told Daybreak.

She haltered Melody and then approached Daybreak. To her surprise, the little filly stood quietly.

"Good girl," Amy praised as she buckled up the halter and slipped the lead-rope through the leather. She rubbed the little foal's head. Daybreak looked at her and then lowered her nose.

"Are you ready?" Ty said, coming into the stall.

Amy nodded. Ty led Melody out and, clicking her tongue, Amy followed with Daybreak.

Daybreak's ears pricked at being outside again. She surged slightly ahead of Amy. "Easy now," Amy said, checking her. As she did so, she tensed, half-expecting Daybreak to explode with indignation, but to her surprise the filly slowed down obediently. "Good girl," Amy praised her in astonishment.

They continued to walk around the yard without incident.

"She was great," Ty said when they put Daybreak and Melody back in their stall ten minutes later.

"I know," Amy said. "She didn't barge or push me or try to rear."

"She's probably still feeling too weak to fight," Ty said.

Amy stared at the filly for a moment. She wasn't sure. She might have been imagining it, but out on the yard it had seemed to her that Daybreak hadn't *wanted* to fight any more. She wondered whether to say anything to Ty and then decided not to. He was probably right. Daybreak was still recovering from a serious illness, no wonder she was being quiet.

* * *

However, over the next few days, as Daybreak regained her strength she also continued to behave. It was too windy for her and Melody to go out and so, twice a day, Ty and Amy led the mare and her little foal round the yard. Not once did Daybreak show any sign of fighting the lead-rope. In fact, not only did she not fight it, but she also seemed willingly to follow Amy on a loose rope wherever Amy wanted to go.

And it wasn't just the leading on the yard. Even in the stall, Amy noticed a change in Daybreak. Although the filly never whinnied to Amy like Melody did, she did whatever Amy asked without trying to resist.

By Friday, two days before Christmas, Amy was convinced that she wasn't imagining the change in the foal. "I'm sure she's getting better-behaved," she said to Ty as they brought Melody and Daybreak back to their stall after one of their yard walks. "Look." She stopped the foal with the lead-rope and, by pressing on her sides, got her to move forwards, sideways and backwards. Daybreak's eyes didn't even flicker. She moved where Amy wanted, responding to the lightest pressure from Amy's hands, her intelligent eyes calm. "She wouldn't have done that before she was ill," Amy said, patting her.

"You're right," Ty admitted. "There is a change in her."

"Why do you think it's happened?" Amy asked.

"Probably has something to do with the virus," Ty said. "She was too weak to run away or fight or kick and so she had to submit to being handled. She became dependent on you and, because you helped her, she's learnt to respect and trust you." He smiled. "I'd never wish any horse to be ill, but I think, in this case, it's really helped."

An image came into Amy's mind of the night she had massaged Daybreak after crying in the stall. She remembered how the resentment in the foal's eyes had gradually faded, and she also remembered the deep feeling of peace that had enveloped her as her fingers worked on and on. Maybe the change in Daybreak had happened then. Who could tell? She stroked the little foal. All that mattered was that she had come to respect and trust them without them needing to force her to.

She and Ty put the mare and foal back into their stall. As they came out of the barn, Ty said, "Have you had any news from Lou?"

"She rang last night," Amy replied. "But the strike's still on." She swallowed. "It's beginning to look like Marnie and I might be having Christmas on our own."

Ty looked at her sympathetically. "Look, why don't I come over — spend the day here with you."

Amy smiled but shook her head. "Thanks, Ty, but your family will want to see you. You're here enough as it is."

"I don't mind," Ty said softly.

Amy's mind suddenly filled with the memory of his birthday. "Marnie and I will be fine," she gabbled, feeling a blush flooding into her cheeks.

Just then, there was the sound of the phone ringing. "I'll get it," Amy said with relief.

She ran down to the kitchen and grabbed the receiver. "Hello, Heartland," she said.

"Hi, Amy, it's me."

"Grandpa!" Amy said in surprise. She felt suddenly worried. "Are you OK? There's nothing wrong, is there?"

"No," Grandpa said. "There's nothing wrong. In fact," Amy heard the smile in his voice, "there's something very right."

"What?" Amy asked.

"The hospital has told me I can come home, Amy. I'll be back for Christmas after all."

Chapter Thirteen

Amy could hardly believe it. "But that's brilliant!" she gasped.

"I know." Grandpa sounded equally amazed. "I've had to promise to take it very easy, of course, but at least I'll be with you."

"So, when can we come and collect you?" Amy said.

"Any time," Grandpa said.

"I can't wait to tell Marnie!" Amy exclaimed. Just then, she saw Marnie's car drawing up outside. "Look, I'd better go," she said, wanting to tell her the good news about Grandpa. "We'll be over to collect you in about an hour."

She put the phone down and ran outside. Marnie grinned madly as Amy told her about Grandpa's call. "That's wonderful news," she cried, and gave Amy a hug.

"What is?" Ben said, turning the water tap off and racing over. "Has Lou got a flight after all?"

Amy shook her head. "No, but Grandpa's coming home!"

"Oh wow!" Ben exclaimed. "So you're *not* going to be on your own for Christmas?"

"No," Amy said, her eyes sparkling with happiness.

Ben smiled. "I was going to offer to stay."

Amy grinned. "Not you as well."

Ben looked confused. "What?"

"It doesn't matter," Amy said. She hugged him. "But you and Ty are the best guys ever!"

Amy set off with Marnie to the hospital. They went in Grandpa's car so there would be more room. When they got there, they found him already waiting with his bag packed.

"Now, you take it easy, Mr Bartlett," Dr Marshall warned, having come to see him off. "And remember your antibiotics."

"I will," Grandpa smiled. "Thank you for everything, Doctor."

"No problem," she said, with a smile. "And we'll see you straight after the holidays for one final check-up."

"I can't believe you're really coming home, Grandpa," Amy said happily as they set off to the car.

"No, neither can I," Grandpa said smiling. "And it's Christmas Eve tomorrow!"

"I'm afraid we haven't really got into the Christmas spirit," Marnie said. "You won't find any decorations up or anything."

"We can soon see to that," Grandpa said.

"Grandpa! Were you listening to what the doctor said? You've got to take it easy," Amy protested.

"Oh, I'm planning to take it easy," Grandpa said, coughing slightly. "But that doesn't mean I can't organize *you* two."

On the way home, he made them stop and buy the biggest Christmas tree they could find.

"I'm glad we brought your car," Marnie said as they struggled to strap it to the roof.

"We can't have Christmas without a tree," Grandpa said.

When they got back, they found that they hadn't been the only ones thinking about Christmas. Ty and Ben had found the battered boxes of old decorations that Grandpa kept in the basement and had set to work making the yard and the house look as festive as possible. Fairy lights flickered along the roof of the front stable, and the kitchen, porch and tack-room had been decorated with Christmas garlands.

"Oh, cool!" Amy said, jumping out of the car.

Ty and Ben came down the yard.

"Welcome home, Jack," Ty said, helping Grandpa out of the car. "It's great to have you back."

Grandpa looked round, a contented smile on his face. "It's good to *be* back," he said.

With Grandpa back at Heartland, the whole house came alive again. He spent the evening supervising Amy and Marnie as they decorated the Christmas tree and put up all the cards that had arrived. Amy tried to ring her sister to tell her that Grandpa was home, but when she spoke to the hotel they said that Miss Fleming had checked out some hours ago. Knowing that Lou had been planning to stay with friends if she didn't get a flight home that day, Amy didn't feel too worried – she just wanted to tell her the good news.

Later that evening, the phone rang. Amy raced to answer it but it wasn't Lou. It was Soraya. "Have you had any news from Lou?" she asked.

"No," Amy replied. "But Grandpa's home from hospital. They discharged him early."

"That's brilliant!" Soraya said.

"I know. I just wish Lou was going to be here too," Amy said. She sighed and then changed the subject. "So, are you coming round tomorrow?" Every Christmas Eve, Soraya came round to help with the horses and they went out for a long trail-ride in the afternoon after the chores were done.

"Of course," Soraya said. "I'll come round just after nine."

"Great," Amy said, pleased. "I'll see you then."

When Amy woke up the next morning, she became aware of a change in the air. She went to the window. There had been another fall of snow overnight. A heavy white blanket covered the fields and trees, and everywhere was quiet and still. The chill wind that had been blowing for the last week or so had finally dropped.

Amy pulled on her clothes and went downstairs. Both

Grandpa and Marnie were still in bed. Taking a few biscuits from the tin on the shelf, she went outside and stood for a moment in the quiet world. *It's Christmas Eve*, she thought, a pleasant tingle of anticipation running down her spine.

Ty and Ben arrived an hour later, at seven o'clock, and they all set to work on the horses. They were mucking out when Marnie came outside with coffee and more biscuits. "I'm going to cook a huge brunch for everyone," she announced, handing Ty and Ben their hot drinks. She grinned at Amy. "It's the only way I can stop your grandpa from doing it."

"Thanks," Amy said gratefully, blowing on her steaming coffee.

"No problem," Marnie replied. "It'll be ready at about ten."

Amy forked the last few pieces of dirty straw from Jake's stall into the wheelbarrow. She was so glad that Grandpa was home for Christmas. *If only Lou were here too*, she thought, *then everything really would be perfect.*

She had just emptied the wheelbarrow when she heard the sound of a car's engine. Thinking it would be Soraya, she ran down the yard. To her surprise, she saw Scott driving up.

"Hi there," Scott said as he got out of his jeep. "I wasn't doing anything this morning so I thought I'd drop by and see if you could use some help with the horses."

"Thanks," Amy said, touched by the gesture.

"How's your grandpa?" Scott asked.

"He's better – in fact, he's here," Amy said, realizing that

Scott wouldn't have heard the news. "He came home last night."

"That's wonderful!" Scott exclaimed. "Is he well enough for me to go in and say hello?"

"I guess so." Amy thought about the way Grandpa had been bossing her and Marnie about the night before and smiled. "I think he's well enough to see you."

Scott went down to the house.

Amy had just started mucking out Sundance's stall when Soraya arrived. She jumped out of her mom's car almost before it had stopped. "Hi!" she said, hugging Amy. "How are you?"

"Great," Amy said, and she realized she meant it.

With Scott and Soraya helping, the mucking out took no time at all. As Amy was finishing Moochie's stall, she became aware that the clouds overhead had parted and that blue sky was showing through.

She went into the next-door stall where Ty was grooming Jake. "Do you think it's warm enough to turn out Melody and Daybreak for a while?"

"Yeah, definitely," Ty said, glancing out of the stall. "Do you want a hand?"

"Thanks," Amy said gratefully. They fetched the mare and foal and led them out through the snow to the paddock beside the house. Daybreak looked round excitedly, her nostrils flaring as she breathed in the crisp, clear air.

However, despite her eagerness to be out in the field, she walked obediently beside Amy.

"She's really improved," Ty said, looking at her.

"Yeah," Amy grinned happily. "She has."

They reached the field gate and unclipped the lead-ropes. With a loud snort, Daybreak trotted out across the snowy grass.

In the centre of the field, she stopped, her beautiful head held high, the tips of her tiny ears almost meeting. For a moment she stood, poised and statue-like, every muscle tense. Then, with a sudden toss of her head, she squealed mischievously and plunged forward in a blur of glowing chestnut, her back legs kicking up a flurry of snowflakes.

Amy's heart swelled with happiness. The little filly might submit willingly to the control of the halter and lead-rope now, but her spirit remained unbroken. She was still fiery, proud and free.

Daybreak wheeled round and cantered towards the gate. Amy expected to see her go over to Melody and drink, but she didn't. Slowing down, she trotted past her mother and stopped and looked at Amy.

Very slowly, wondering what she wanted, Amy stepped into the field and held out her hand. "Here, girl," she said softly.

Daybreak hesitated and then, with the faintest of whickers, she walked forward. Stretching her head out, she nuzzled Amy's upturned palm. Then, lifting her tiny muzzle to Amy's face, she breathed out warmly, love and trust glowing in her dark eyes.

Triumph and delight surged through Amy's veins. Daybreak's fight was over. Suddenly all the frustration and sleepless nights that the foal had caused her were forgotten. Breathing in the sweet scent of Daybreak's breath, she kissed the little filly's nose.

"Daybreak," she whispered softly. "My Daybreak."

The moment was shattered by the sound of the back door opening and Marnie calling out. "Brunch is ready, everyone!"

With a swift toss of her head, Daybreak plunged away.

Amy turned and met Ty's eyes.

"You've done it, Amy," he said softly. "You've won her trust."

Amy's face glowed as she went over to the gate. "We did it together," she said, knowing that she could never have done it without him.

He smiled at her and they went down to the house together.

The kitchen table was piled high with food – there were dishes of crispy bacon, grilled sausages and golden scrambled eggs, two huge bowls of fresh fruit salad, a platter of steaming blueberry pancakes, two jugs of maple syrup and a mountain of freshly baked muffins and cinnamon rolls.

"Sit down, everyone," Marnie said as they all kicked off their boots.

"Wow!" Ben said, looking round. "This is some spread."

Grandpa was sitting at the head of the table. "Who wants coffee?"

"I'll do that, Jack," Scott said, taking the coffee pot off him. "You just sit there and enjoy."

Talking and laughing, everybody pulled chairs up to the table.

"This is incredible, Marnie," Amy said as she carried a pile of warmed plates to the table.

"Thanks," Marnie replied. "Jack instructed me from the armchair!"

Amy put the plates down on the table. "Now, everyone help themselves," she said, handing them out.

She had just sat down between Ty and Soraya when the back door suddenly opened.

Amy jumped to her feet and turned round. "Lou!" she exclaimed.

A silence fell on the room. Lou stood in the doorway. Her hair was dishevelled and her face was tired. She was looking round in astonishment at the crowded kitchen. "What's ... what's going on?" Then her eyes fell on Grandpa. "Grandpa!" she gasped. "You're home!"

She dropped her bag and ran to him. He rose to meet her. "Oh Lou, it's so good to see you! But we weren't expecting you for ages."

"I got a flight!" Lou said. "The strike was suddenly called off. I couldn't ring – there was no time. I just had to get on that plane and come home. But what about you, Grandpa?"

she said, pulling back from him. "I thought you'd still be in hospital."

"They let me come home yesterday," Grandpa said.

"On strict instructions that he takes it easy," smiled Amy, butting in.

"I've been so worried about you," Lou exclaimed. "Leaving here while you were so ill was the stupidest idea I've ever had. I don't know what possessed me."

"But I made you go, Lou," Grandpa said, reaching for her hand.

"Only because you knew how important it was to me," Lou said sadly. "I *thought* I wanted to go, but being away from here and not being able to get back when I was needed was a nightmare." She sighed deeply. "I was blind to anything else but finding Daddy... Please forgive me."

Jack smiled. "There's nothing to forgive," he said.

"But there is," Lou insisted. "I was really selfish." She turned to her sister. "I should have been here to help while Grandpa was ill instead of running away to London. It must have been terrible for you. I'm so sorry, Amy."

"It doesn't matter any more," Amy said, hugging her in delight. "I'm just glad you're back."

"You don't know how glad I am to *be* back. Being away made me realize a lot of things..." Lou paused. "I can't go on waiting for Daddy any more – I know that's a mistake; we'll meet up soon enough. There are more important things for me here." Lou smiled and looked across the room at Scott.

"This is my home now."

Scott stood up. "Do you really mean that, Lou?"

Lou went over to him. "Yes," she said. "I do." She took his hands, her eyes searching his face. "Scott, I can't believe how I treated you — it was so rude and unforgivable. I can be so stubborn sometimes. You know I didn't..."

Before Lou could apologize any further, Scott wrapped his arms around her in a bear hug. "It doesn't matter, Lou. I know you didn't mean it... I've missed you so much," he whispered into her hair.

"I've missed you too," Lou said, half-laughing, half-crying. "I'll make it up to everyone, I promise."

Amy sank down in her chair, her legs feeling suddenly shaky. Lou was back. Now *everyone* was home for Christmas.

Just then, the phone rang. Marnie picked it up. "Hello — Heartland."

She looked at Lou, frowning. "Lou," she said. Amy couldn't help notice a strange tone in her voice. "It's for you."

"Can you tell them I'll ring them back," Lou said, turning happily in Scott's arms.

"Well ... it's a long-distance call," Marnie said. "It's ... it's from Australia."

Lou's face suddenly paled. "Australia?" she whispered.

Marnie nodded. "It's your father."

"You don't have to speak to him, Lou," Amy said quickly. "You..."

But Lou had already pulled away from Scott and taken the

phone. "Hello," she said, her voice catching in her throat. "Daddy?"

She turned and walked out of the room and into the hall, shutting the door behind her.

No one spoke. Amy looked at Grandpa. His face was tense.

After five minutes, the door opened and Lou came back in. Amy's eyes flew to her sister's face. She was even paler than before and her blue eyes looked shocked. She handed the receiver to Amy. "He ... he wants to speak to you," she said, her voice now low and wavering.

Amy shook her head frantically, but Lou shoved the receiver in her hand and walked away to the sink. For a moment Amy didn't know what to do, but then, very slowly, she lifted the phone to her ear. "Hello?" she whispered, turning away from everyone in the room.

"Hello, Amy." The strange English voice on the other end of the line seemed unfamiliar at first but, deep in the corners of Amy's mind, a long-forgotten memory stirred. She wanted to speak but just couldn't.

"I guess you don't remember me that well."

"No," Amy said, her heart beating fast.

"Well, I remember you," her father said, his voice warm. "In fact, I've got a photo of you in my wallet. You and Lou at the seaside. I carry it on me all the time."

Amy didn't know what to say. For twelve years, her father had been absent from her life and now, suddenly, here he was, speaking to her on the telephone.

Her father seemed to feel the awkwardness of the situation too. "Look, I'm sorry for ringing out of the blue like this," he said. "I'd rather have met you face to face after all this time, but when I heard from the Carters that Lou had been to England to find me, I knew that I had to ring from Australia and explain."

Amy was silent.

"I live on a large farm here," her father went on. "I raise horses. Lou said in her letter that you're really into horses. You'd like it here."

Amy didn't say anything. Suddenly, she heard the sound of a baby crying in the background. "Is that a baby?" she asked.

"Yes," her father said. There was a pause. "My wife gave birth to our little girl last week."

For a second, the world seemed to stop. The words ran through Amy's head. *Wife. Baby.* She looked at Lou's back and immediately understood the shocked look she had seen in her sister's eyes.

"I just explained to Lou that that's why I can't meet you until February," their father carried on. "I need to be here at the moment. It's also why I didn't tell you that I'm living in Australia. I thought the news that I'd remarried and that you had a half-sister might be better coming face to face."

"I understand," Amy whispered.

There was a silence.

"Look, I think I'd better give you a little time to let all this news sink in," her father said. "There's much more that we need to talk about, but that can wait. I'll call again after the holidays, if that's OK? For now, let me just wish you a happy Christmas, Amy, and I look forward to seeing you in the new year."

"O-OK," Amy stammered. "Bye, Daddy."

As Amy put the phone down, Lou turned and met her eyes. Her face was wet with tears.

"What did your father say?" Grandpa asked, looking anxious.

Amy looked round, her head spinning. "That he's married and they've just had a baby girl."

She saw the shock register on everyone's face.

"A baby!" Grandpa echoed. He stood up, his face suddenly ashen. "Lou..."

"I'm all right," Lou interrupted. She lifted her head and brushed the tears away from her eyes. "I'm ... I'm *glad* that Daddy's found some happiness at last."

"Do you mean that?" Grandpa said.

"Yes," Lou replied, going to Scott's side and taking his hand. "Daddy's got his life now and I've got mine. And it's here at Heartland with all of you." Tears still glistened in her eyes, but she smiled and breathed in deeply. "Now, I don't know about everyone else, but I'm starving," she said. "Are any of those eggs for me?"

It didn't take long to reheat the food. Soon everyone was

sitting down, passing the dishes round and tucking in. As the noise level rose, Amy thought about everything that had happened in the last six months – there had been so much grief, so much pain and so many tears.

But not everything that has happened has been bad, she thought, looking at Ben and Marnie laughing with Soraya. New friends had been made and old friendships strengthened. *And not just friendships*, she thought, her eyes looking to Lou. For so much of her life, her sister had been almost like a stranger to her, but over the last six months a new bond had been forged between them. Now they didn't just love each other, they understood and needed each other too.

As Amy finished the last piece of muffin on her plate, Ty touched her arm. "We should probably bring Melody and Daybreak in. We don't want that little foal getting a chill."

Amy nodded and they stood up.

"You're not going back out just yet, are you?" Lou said to them. "I was just going to make some fresh coffee."

"We'll be back soon," Amy replied, smiling at her big sister. "We're just going to put Melody and Daybreak back inside."

She and Ty pulled on their boots and left the warmth of the house. After the laughter and noise of the kitchen, the yard held a soothing silence for them both. Only the occasional snort of one of the horses in the stalls broke into the calm.

"Look," Ty said, pointing to the field.

Amy smiled. Melody and Daybreak were standing by the water trough. The foal was suckling, her fluffy tail switching from side to side as Melody gently nuzzled her hindquarters. The rays of the winter sun shone down on their backs.

Amy and Ty stopped by the gate.

"Don't they look peaceful?" Ty said.

Amy nodded and leant against the gate. "Everywhere's so quiet," she said softly.

"For once." Ty's eyes met hers. "It's been a tough six months, Amy."

"Yeah ... but it's been good too," Amy said. "Lou's come back to live here, Grandpa's on the mend, Heartland's still helping horses and I know I've got the best friends and family in the world." She looked up at Ty, knowing he'd understand. "I still miss Mom and Pegasus – I always will – but I can never bring them back. It's time to move on." She paused for a moment and watched the mare and filly in the field. When she spoke again, her voice was quiet. "You remember how Mom used to say, 'One day you'll know when the good times are here'?"

Ty nodded.

"Well, I had some wonderful times *with* Mom," Amy said slowly. "But now I know I've got to find my own good times. It's ... it's what Mom would have wanted."

"Yes," Ty said softly. "It is."

Amy met his gaze. She didn't know what she'd have done

without him over the last six months. "Thank you," she said suddenly.

"What for?" Ty asked, looking surprised.

"For being here," Amy said. "For helping me." She saw him about to speak – to shrug it off – but she shook her head, wanting to tell him how much he meant to her. "If it hadn't been for you, Ty, Heartland wouldn't exist any more. You're so important to this place ... and to me."

"And you're important to me, Amy," Ty said warmly. He stepped closer. "Very important."

Amy felt her stomach somersault as she looked up at him. "Ty?" she said, as his hands touched her shoulders.

But Ty didn't speak. His eyes looked deep into hers and then his lips met her own.

Amy didn't know how long the kiss lasted. But when it stopped, her heart was pounding so hard she thought it was going to burst. "Ty?" she stammered.

Ty looked down at her and smiled. "Happy Christmas, Amy," he said. "I hope those good times come soon."

Amy glanced at Melody and Daybreak then round at the house. Through the kitchen windows, with their festive decorations, she could see everyone she loved most in the world gathered together. "They're here already," she said, looking back at Ty. "They really are."

She opened the field gate. Daybreak whinnied and, with a smile, Amy walked across the snow towards the little foal.

Read the first book about

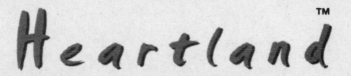

book one

Coming Home

The truck splashed along the rutted driveway. Marion stopped it outside the house and jumped out, leaving the headlights on to illuminate their way. Amy grabbed the halter and lead-rope from the seat beside her while Marion put the trailer ramp down. "Which building is it?" she called to Amy.

"That one!" Amy shouted, raising her voice above the wind.

They staggered through the rain to the barn. After Marion had pulled back the bolts, they heaved the door open together so it stood slightly ajar. Amy looked in. The bay stallion stared at them, head up, nostrils flaring, eyes wild. Marion looked at him for a moment and then turned her back to the wind and took out a small container from her pocket. From inside, she took a pinch of dark, gritty dust and rubbed it into her hands. "Stand back a bit," she said softly to Amy.

Amy did as she was told and Marion squeezed through the gap in the door. The horse moved uneasily on the spot, his ears back. Turning herself sideways on to him, Marion looked at the floor. The stallion regarded her warily. Very slowly she held out her hand. The bay made to jerk his head back but then he seemed to suddenly catch the scent of the powder. His nostrils flared and he inhaled, his ears suddenly pricking up.

Amy held her breath. The powder was made from chestnut trimmings which were insensitive, horny growths found on the inside of horses' front legs. An old horseman had once taught Marion that the scent would calm nervous and frightened horses. Now, sheltering in the doorway, Amy watched to see what would happen.

Very cautiously, the horse stretched out his head. Marion stayed absolutely still, eyes averted. *I am no threat*, her body language seemed to be saying. The horse took a step forward, all the time breathing in. His delicate muzzle touched Marion's hand, his nostrils dilating. He took another step forward and lifted his head to her hair, breathing in and then out.

Very slowly, Amy saw her mom turn, and as the stallion breathed in again the fear left his eyes. His muscles relaxed and he lowered his head to nuzzle Marion's hand. She stroked him. "Pass me the halter," she said quietly to Amy.

Without the slightest objection, the horse let Marion slip on the halter. She patted him. "Come on, boy, let's get you into the trailer."

Amy heaved the door open. The horse obediently followed Marion out into the sheeting rain. Amy patted him and he nuzzled her arm. Now his initial fear was gone he seemed friendly, even affectionate.

When they reached the trailer she stood on the ramp and rattled a feed bucket. The horse stretched out his head and neck and gobbled a mouthful. Then, with no more prompting, he walked calmly into the box. Amy put down the bucket to let him eat and then, leaving her mom to tie him up, she slipped out of the side door to pull up the ramp. Her wet fingers slipped as she fastened the bolts. The wind and rain lashed down. At last Marion emerged. "Home," she said, coming round to check the bolts. "And fast."

Their faces were streaming with water as they climbed back into the truck. Marion turned the key and the engine spluttered into life. Amy shivered and squeezed water from her hair. Marion turned on the heater. It roared noisily, competing with the sound of the rain. They could hear the stallion move uneasily in the back as the rain battered the roof of the trailer.

Outside there was an ominous rumbling. Seconds later, a jagged fork of lightning split the sky and the rain started to sheet down with a new intensity. As they turned on to the steep road downwards, a crash of thunder broke over them.

The horse began to panic. His feet thudded against the side of the box, causing it to rock alarmingly. Amy glanced anxiously at her mother. The truck was gathering speed as it headed down the hill. Marion was concentrating hard, braking slowly and steadily to keep the trailer under control on the wet road.

"This is insane," muttered Marion. "I should never have let you talk me into this, Amy." Her eyes showed her anxiety as she gripped the steering wheel tightly.

Amy jumped as lightning forked straight down through the sky accompanied by an immense clap of thunder. The stallion's hooves crashed into the walls of the trailer again and again as he struggled to escape from his moving prison.

The tunnel of dark trees loomed up ahead. As they entered, branches closed over the top of the trailer, banging and scraping against it. Every muscle in Amy's body was tense. Her heart was pounding. Her breath was short in her throat.

The trees on each side of them swayed as the unrelenting wind and rain bent them against their will. The road seemed pitch-black beneath the tree canopy. Then there was a brilliant flash of lightning and a clap of thunder so loud it sounded as if a cannon had gone off overhead. Amy screamed and jumped. The horse let out a shriek as a cracking noise echoed through the tunnel.

Straight in front of them, a tree started to fall.

Marion braked violently but the tyres failed to grip the flooded surface. The truck skidded down the road, straight into the path of the tree.

Time slowed down. Powerless to do anything, Amy watched as the tree fell in horrifyingly slow motion towards them. For one wild moment she thought they were just going to get past, but then with a final creaking, crashing noise, the tree collapsed.

With startling clarity, in a single second that seemed to last for ever, Amy saw every little detail, every vein of every green, damp leaf. "*Mom!*" she screamed.

There was a bang, a sickening feeling of falling, and then nothing.